BATTLE CRY AT BATOCHE

BATTLE CRY AT BATOCHE

a novel by

B. J. BAYLE

An imprint of
Beach Holme Publishing
Vancouver

First Edition

05 04 03 02 01 00 5 4 3 2 1

This book is published by Beach Holme Publishing, 226-2040 West 12th Avenue, Vancouver, B.C. V6J 2G2. This is a Porcepic Book.

The publisher gratefully acknowledges the financial support of the Canada Council for the Arts and of the British Columbia Arts Council. The publisher also acknowledges the financial assistance received from the Government of Canada through the Book Publishing Industry Development Program (BPIDP) for its publishing activities.

Editor: Michael Carroll
Production and Design: Jen Hamilton
Cover Art: Tilly Milton

Printed and bound in Canada by Marc Veilleux Imprimeur

Canadian Cataloguing in Publication Data

Bayle, B. J. (Beverly J.)
Battle cry at Batoche

"A sandcastle book."
ISBN 0-88878-414-7

I. Title.
PS8553.A943B37 2000 jC813'.54 C00-910656-1
PZ7.B34Ba 2000

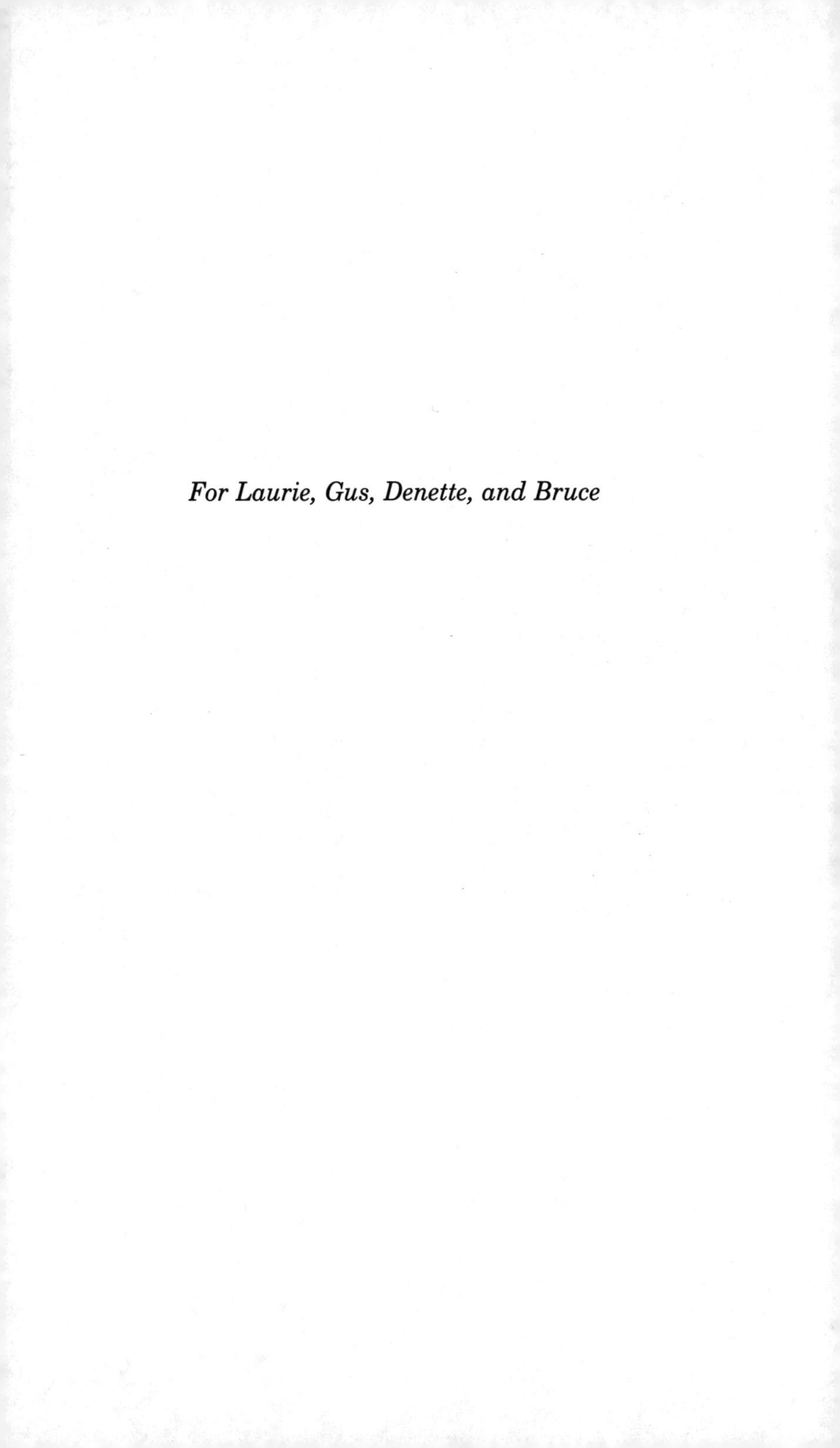

For Laurie, Gus, Denette, and Bruce

ACKNOWLEDGEMENTS

First and foremost, my thanks to my husband, Hank Bayle, for enthusiastic help with my research. Thanks also to Neil Colvin for the loan of his five-volume set of *The Collected Writings of Louis Riel* and to Lois Patterson for sharing books, documents, and news clippings concerning the Canadian military during the North-West Rebellion.

I also owe thanks to the impressive Hudson's Bay Archives in Winnipeg for the detailed accounts of the lives of some of those involved in the events leading to the 1885 conflict. And I certainly must express my appreciation for the wealth of information at Saskatchewan's Duck Lake Historical Museum, and also for the splendid reconstruction of the Fort Carlton Hudson's Bay trading post. Thanks, too, to the friendly staff in Calgary's Glenbow Museum for their help in locating pictures of the players in the bitter struggle at Batoche.

This book would not have been written were it not for the impressive Batoche National Historic Park. It is a quiet landscape of rolling hills covered with dry, waving grass where wagon ruts still mark the Carlton Trail and indentations pit the earth where desperate men defended their land. The information centre there is superb, and the staff are friendly and helpful.

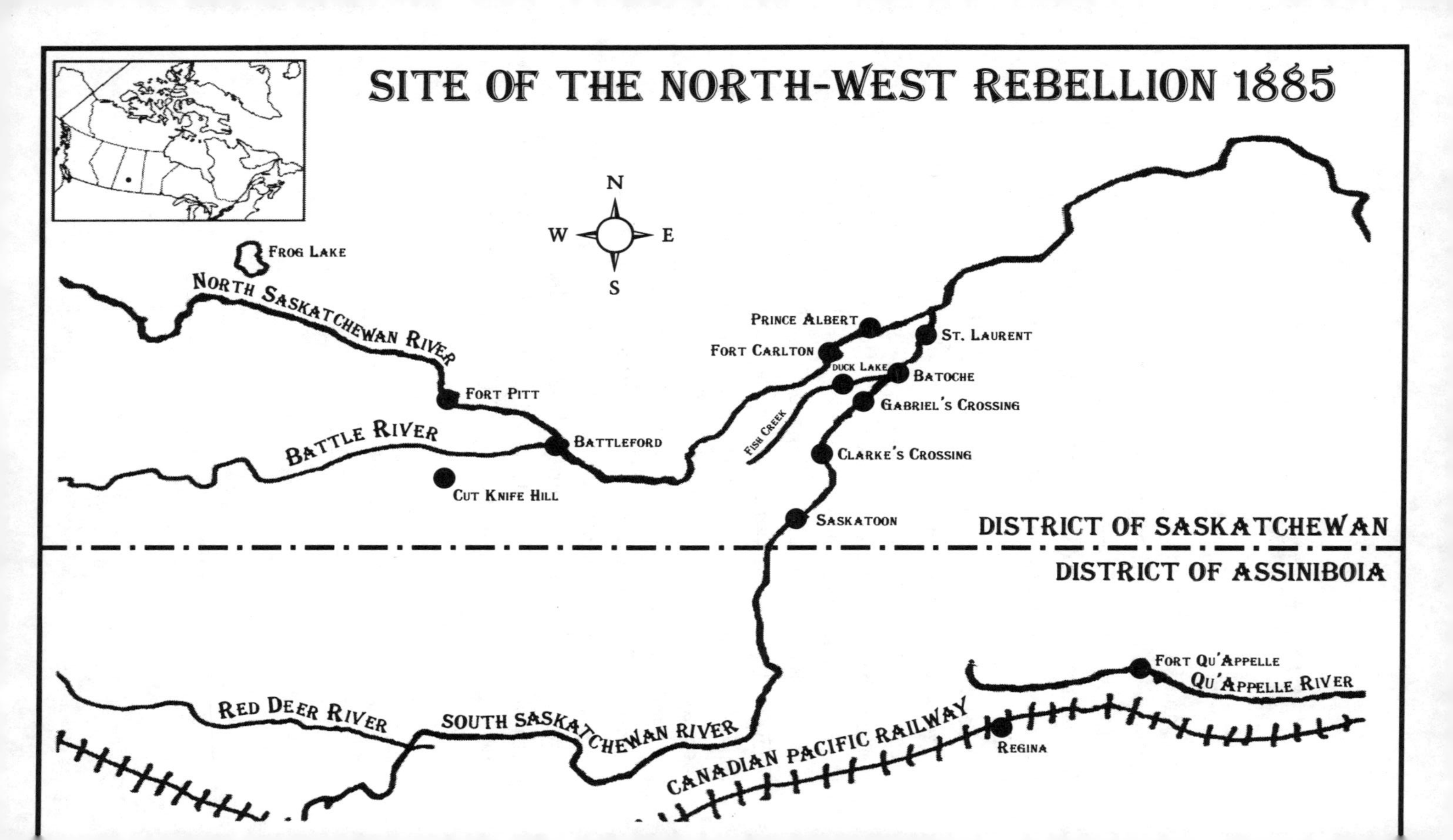
SITE OF THE NORTH-WEST REBELLION 1885
N
W
E
S
FROG LAKE
NORTH SASKATCHEWAN RIVER
FORT PITT
BATTLE RIVER
BATTLEFORD
CUT KNIFE HILL
PRINCE ALBERT
FORT CARLTON
DUCK LAKE
ST. LAURENT
BATOCHE
GABRIEL'S CROSSING
FISH CREEK
CLARKE'S CROSSING
SASKATOON
DISTRICT OF SASKATCHEWAN
DISTRICT OF ASSINIBOIA
FORT QU'APPELLE
QU'APPELLE RIVER
RED DEER RIVER
SOUTH SASKATCHEWAN RIVER
CANADIAN PACIFIC RAILWAY
REGINA

ONE

Ben Muldoon trudged head down through the shallow ravine, not caring that his footsteps had splintered the silence of the sun-dappled forest all the way to the river. As he tugged at the reins of the tall black horse plodding behind him, he wished he hadn't left the main trail to follow this game track. He slapped at a cloud of tiny insects in front of his face and considered climbing back on his horse again, though each time he did, the low branches of spruce and cottonwood knocked off his flat-crowned black hat and scraped his face. No matter. He would be at the river soon enough.

Rounding a sharp turn in the trail, he froze as a blast from a gun reverberated in the stillness. In the same instant a bullet whistled past his ear. Dropping to his knees, Ben released his hold on the reins and, with shaking hands, steadied his rifle. He peered into the forest around him, his heart hammering and the inside of his mouth suddenly as dry as yesterday's bannock. A twig snapped, but he turned too late. With the shove from behind, he lost his grip on his rifle. When he sprawled face forward, a brown hand reached for the gun. Fear galvanized Ben as he leaped up and lunged at his assailant. Dry branches of brush snapped as the two boys grappled and fell to the ground. In a moment it was over.

It was almost too easy, but as Ben looked down, he realized the Indian pinned to the ground was probably no older than himself and about twenty pounds lighter. He got to his feet slowly and backed away a few steps before bending to pick up his rifle. His eyes on his captive, he worked the lever to send a cartridge into the breech. "Get up."

His prisoner lay still, eyeing him warily. Ben repeated his command, this time in halting French. The boy turned on his side and closed his eyes. Astonishment made Ben forget his anger. "Here now," he commanded, prodding a leg with the butt of his gun, "you've rested enough. Get up."

The silence in the forest lengthened, and for the first time it occurred to Ben they might not be alone. Perhaps the Indian was waiting for somebody. Ben darted quick glances over each shoulder, then turned back to find the boy watching him. Scowling, he jerked his thumb upward. This time the boy sat up cross-legged and stared at him. Satisfied he was making progress, Ben repeated his gesture, but his captive shook his head. "You will say I tried to steal your rifle, and I will be locked in a dirty jail."

"Well, what did you expect?" Ben retorted. "I oughta say 'better luck next time' and let you go after you tried to kill me?"

There was no humour in the other boy's smile. "If I had meant to kill you, you would not be speaking now."

"You saying you didn't try? I guess your gun just went off accidental like."

"My shot was for a deer—an easy target until you came with more noise than a bear rolling downhill. Even so it is wounded."

"Then why didn't you follow the deer instead of jumping on me?"

A fleeting look of hopelessness crossed the Indian's face before he muttered, "I have no more powder and shot."

As he surveyed his captive, Ben thought he understood why losing the deer made him crazy enough to attack. Sun-browned skin outlined each rib and covered the boy's arms as though there were nothing between it and bone. The skin stretched tightly over hollows under high cheekbones jutting beneath dark, deep-set eyes that glittered with anger now, as if they understood Ben's unexpected flash of pity and rejected it.

Ben strode to his waiting horse and said gruffly, "Well, come on. You can't shoot a deer and leave it to bleed to death." When the boy hesitated, Ben grabbed the reins and started off in what he hoped was the right direction. Over his shoulder he called, "Come on!" Then he halted and turned. "Say, what's your name, anyway? I like to know who I'm hunting with."

Scrambling to his feet, the boy answered, "Red Eagle."

"Come on then, Red Eagle. Which way do we find the deer?"

"I will get my horse" came the reply, and Red Eagle disappeared into the forest without a sound.

As Ben leaned against a tree and waited, a nagging uneasiness plagued him. It wasn't the same worry that had knotted his stomach the day before when he left Gabriel's Crossing for Fort Carlton. Then, certain his uncle must have returned to the fort, he had rehearsed over and over his explanation for taking his sister to Gabriel Dumont's cabin. Even so, his uncle had been plenty mad until he learned Ben and Charity had had nothing to do with Dumont himself these past two months. That knowledge had caused Lawrence Clarke's fury to be replaced by thoughtful contemplation as he rubbed the red tip of his long, thin nose and studied his nephew with pale blue eyes. Remembering now the relief he had felt when he thought his uncle's anger had passed, Ben grimaced. He didn't know then just what his uncle was planning.

Ben's thoughts flew back to the present as the steady beat of hoofs reached his ears. In a moment Red Eagle was beside him, sliding off a weary dark brown horse. The Indian gestured over his shoulder. "A small stream runs down to the river. We will tie the horses there and follow the deer on foot."

Under a mound of leaves and brush near where they tied the horses, Ben hid the old cap-and-ball musket Red Eagle carried, while the Indian moved through the trees and pointed at the ground. "Here," he said.

Ben pushed aside a bramble of wild rosebushes and saw the telltale splatter of blood. Together they moved through the woods, Red Eagle leading.

It was late afternoon when they found the exhausted animal drinking from a brackish backwater, dried blood caked on one front leg. Ben felt a surge of excitement as he lifted his rifle. Glancing beside him, he saw the eagerness on his companion's face. "Take it," he whispered, abruptly thrusting the rifle into Red Eagle's hands. "It's your deer."

The Enfield spoke once, and the buck dropped. "Good shot," Ben said when they reached the animal. "Right behind the ear."

Red Eagle dropped to his knees and whipped out a long knife from the sheath strapped to his deerskin leggings. Once, as he prepared the deer for travel, he sliced off a thin strip of meat and popped it into his mouth, chewing hungrily as he worked. His upward glance caught the disgust on Ben's face, and he scowled. "It is not so easy to wait to cook meat when you have none for three months!"

Ben said nothing. He knew by heart Uncle Lawrence's speech about the Indians being hungry because they expected to be fed instead of raising their food on land the government had been good enough to give them. Even his uncle had to admit, though, that some of the white men hired to teach the Indians how to farm weren't very helpful.

Although he had been raised to accept the judgements of his elders as gospel, Ben had a vague feeling of embarrassment as he watched the scrawny figure work over the deer. Impulsively he reached inside his grey homespun shirt for a package wrapped in oiled paper and held it out. "Here," he said. "If you still got an appetite, you'd do me a favour if you eat this." When the boy hesitated, Ben added, "I already had my fill, and the woman who wrapped that up likely might think I'm sick if I bring it back."

Ben had expected Red Eagle to wolf down the bannock and meat, but the boy chewed slowly, surveying Ben as he ate. Between bites he said, "You are far from Fort Carlton."

Ben's brow furrowed. "How'd you know I been at Fort Carlton?"

The reply was slow in coming. "Three months ago I took wolf skins to the fort to trade for flour. You are called Ben Muldoon, but in our camp you are known as Fire on Top."

Ben was accustomed to comments about his unruly mop of bright red hair. It was too curly to trim neatly in the fashion of young men, so he was content to clip it off below his ears and let it blow freely. He grinned as he said, "That's as good a name as any, I guess. But I don't live at the fort anymore—at least for now. I've been staying at Gabriel's Crossing for the past while. I rode to the fort today to see my uncle, and I'm on my way back."

Red Eagle stared at Ben thoughtfully for a moment before he bent over the deer again. "So," he said over his shoulder, "you share the cabin of Gabriel Dumont."

Half wondering why he should bother to explain himself to an Indian, Ben said, "My sister got real sick at the fort, and some said I best take her to Madame Dumont. The Mounted Police took us over to the Crossing in a wagon a while back."

Red Eagle nodded without turning around. "My people know of her also. She has healing hands."

"I expect so," Ben said, recalling the nights he had awakened to see the Métis woman dozing in a chair by his sister's bed. "All I know is, Charity's doing just fine now, but Madame Dumont says I shouldn't take her back to the fort yet." He half suspected she had become pretty fond of Charity and was making excuses to keep her as long as she could. He sighed. Truth to tell, Ben had hated having to tell his sister that their uncle might make them return to the fort when he got back from his trip to Winnipeg. At Gabriel's Crossing Ben heard her laughter for the first time since their mother had died in 1882 almost two years ago.

Red Eagle stood. "I will get the horses."

Ben surveyed the deer. "Where you taking it?"

The Indian jerked his head in a westerly direction. "A day's ride."

"That so? Which reserve you from?"

"Poundmaker's."

Ben whistled under his breath. "You're a ways from home then."

Red Eagle scowled. "Deer are few where we are told to hunt. White—"

"Hey!" Ben interrupted. "I just mean you got more'n a day's ride."

"My companions hunt, as well. We will meet upstream where the north branch of the river bends to the south, and return to Cut Knife together."

"I know the place." Ben squinted at the sun. "It'll take you most of the night to get there. Why don't you come back to Gabriel's Crossing and start out in the morning? I don't guess Gabriel Dumont would mind if you hang your deer in the ice shed."

Some of the stiffness seemed to leave Red Eagle's face. "It is Gabriel Dumont who told me there are deer in these woods."

"Well, come on, then. It'll save time if we pack this thing back to the horses." As Ben bent to pick up one end of the deer, he felt oddly lighthearted.

Although Ben was big for his age and had inherited a powerful build from his Irish father, it wasn't easy to get the inert carcass through the woods and slung across the back of Red Eagle's horse. By the time they reached their destination, both boys were spattered with drops of blood, and the moccasin boots they wore were splashed with mud from the banks of the South Saskatchewan River when they crossed it upstream from Gabriel's Crossing.

The door of the long whitewashed log cabin opened as they approached, and Madeleine Dumont called out a greeting, her strong, plain face transformed by her smile. It seemed to Ben that Tante Madeleine was different from most of the vivacious, chattering Métis women he had met. For one thing, she was taller, and her hair was somewhere between light and dark brown—the way his mother's had been. Except for Charity, Ben liked her better than anybody. He knew no matter how hard he tried he would never be able to pay her back for saving his sister's life. To show his gratitude to Tante Madeleine, he helped her whenever he could by looking after the herd of cattle and a half-dozen horses and by cutting hay for their winter feed. Doing it made him feel good; it was like being back on the farm by the Red River.

Tante Madeleine touched the deer. "You did well."

Ben hastened to explain. "It's not mine. It's his."

"We will share," Red Eagle said.

Tante Madeleine didn't reply, but Ben guessed she would find a way to refuse the deer without offending Red Eagle, even though their own supply of meat was low. Six times he had helped her carry food from her storehouse to those along the river who were too old or too ill to hunt for themselves. Had he known there might be deer so close to the village, he would have slipped through the forest more quietly and kept a better watch.

Ben peered behind the woman at the empty doorway. "Where's Charity?"

"The Vanda children came by to hear her stories. They are down by the river." The words were accompanied by a smile.

"We had our meal. After you attend to the deer and your horses, go down and wash. Yours will be ready."

In silence they hung the deer from a beam in the shed before they turned the horses into the grassy pasture beside the stable and loped down the slope to the river. Near the rushing water, Ben veered sideways to a calm backwash and dropped to his knees, gasping with the shock of the icy water as he doused his hands and face. Although the sunny autumn day had been warm, the river was uncomfortably cold. Beside him, Red Eagle dipped his entire head in, then raised it suddenly, alert as a wild thing as he stared around, listening.

The murmur of voices drifted from upstream, and soft laughter, like the tinkling of a bell. "That's my sister," Ben explained. Pulling his shirt free from his dark corduroy trousers, he dried his face. "I'll go tell her I'm back."

Without inviting Red Eagle to accompany him, Ben clambered over the rocks along the shore until he reached a small clearing in the willow bushes clustered along the riverbank. Charity sat under an old spruce tree, one small, fat Métis child in her lap and four others in a half circle around her. Her hair, red as his own, but shot with gold, gave off sparks in the light of the setting sun. Ben noted that Madame Dumont had made yet another new dress for her. Below the heavy black cloak, the folds of her long skirt were spread on the grass. Its colour matched her eyes—blue as his own. But his eyes could see, and Charity's could not.

He turned his head when he heard a sharp intake of breath behind him, ready with a retort if the Cree boy commented on his sister's blindness. But Red Eagle was speechless, his mouth half open as he stared raptly at the girl. Ben moved forward, pausing as he felt a hand on his arm. "She is real?" the boy asked softly.

Ben's mood changed. "Sure enough," he said with a grin. He reckoned even an Indian couldn't help but take in how pretty Charity was. Ben was proud of his twin.

"Ben!" Charity called, turning her head in their direction. "You're late. Did you see Uncle? Is he very angry? Must we go back to the fort?"

"I sure did, and it's all right. We can stay a while longer," Ben said as he strode forward to lift the child from her lap. "Tell you about it later. Tante Madeleine's waiting with our supper."

"Someone is with you?"

Pulling his sister to her feet, Ben said, "An Indian named Red Eagle."

A dimple appeared in one cheek as Charity smiled. "Hello, Red Eagle."

The Cree said nothing. As far as Ben could tell, Red Eagle didn't plan to do anything but stare.

Later, between spoonfuls of potage thick with potatoes and chicken, Ben explained why he was so late, but omitted he had first become acquainted with Red Eagle in a fight.

"I'm glad you found the poor thing, since it was wounded in the leg," Charity said. "Else it would suffer. Is it very big?"

"Big enough so the horse had a hard time carrying it." Ben frowned at Red Eagle, who hadn't taken his eyes off Charity. "Haven't you ever seen a white girl before?"

Red Eagle glanced sideways at Ben. "I have seen many white girls."

Charity turned her head in Red Eagle's direction. "Red Eagle! You do speak English. I thought—" She broke off, her face turning pink.

"Four years I was in a white school," Red Eagle said softly.

Ben hadn't thought to ask how his companion spoke such good English, and he looked at Red Eagle with interest. "Why was that?"

"I was taken into the lodge of Poundmaker. He sent his son and me to the school at Prince Albert."

Tante Madeleine interrupted. "Poundmaker wished them to learn the ways of the white men in the hope they could find a way to keep them from starving and cheating their people."

Ben looked at the woman, surprised by her bitter tone. Her father was a Scottish trader from Fort Ellice and her mother was only half Indian, yet she sounded as though she was all on their side. Something prodded his memory, and for a moment he heard his own mother's gentle voice raised in protest when his father spoke against the Indians. One more way she and Tante Madeleine were alike.

Ben cleared his throat. "How d'you mean, *cheating*?"

"Is it not clear to everyone?" Red Eagle asked. "The Canadians sign treaties they do not keep. It was said we would have seed and ploughs and a man who would teach us to farm well. If not enough food could be grown, they promised we would be given enough for the winter. For three years we have drought and many burrowing animals to eat the crops before we could gather them. The winters are hard and the people are in rags. The old and the children die because they are cold and without food. We hunt though there is nothing left to hunt, so it remains for us to cut wood to sell to the white people. Or beg from them."

A hint of tears edged Charity's voice. "Couldn't you ask for more food from the agents?"

"My people are allowed only a little flour and bacon, but not enough. When I learned there was hunger, I returned."

Ben spoke slowly. "I remember a while back my uncle—Lawrence Clarke—sent a telegram to Ottawa to tell the government the people on the reserves should be better fed."

He didn't mention that his uncle had also said, "Or else they'll listen to the Métis who want to make trouble." But Uncle Lawrence was ignored and a message was sent to the Indian agent ordering him to threaten to cut the allotment for any Indian band that seemed rebellious. Maybe Poundmaker's band had caused trouble. A glance at his sister's unhappy expression told Ben it was time to speak of other things.

"Charity," he said, "what was the story you were telling the—" But he broke off as the sound of hoof beats, muffled at first, rapidly grew louder.

Tante Madeleine sprang to her feet, a smile lighting her face. "Gabriel," she murmured, flinging open the door.

Six men crowded into the room, the one who led the way towering over the rest. He wore dark blue trousers stuffed into deerskin boots laced to his knees, with a blue shirt covered by a bright red vest. His long, thick hair and bushy beard were streaked with grey, but his dark, shining eyes and wide grin gave him a youthful look. He snatched up Tante Madeleine as though she were a child and swung her around. "*Bonsoir*, my treasure!" he boomed. "I have missed you, my lady." Gabriel Dumont put down his wife. Then, keeping one arm around her waist, he raised his head to sniff the air. "I hope you have plenty of your good chicken potage, for we are hungry enough to devour even the big ears of John A. Macdonald."

There followed a volley of French too rapid for Ben to understand, though he sensed the rest of the men protested the offer of a meal. Beside him at the long table, Charity clutched his arm and said, "Ben, I hear many different voices. Do they all live here? Will there still be room for us?"

A lump rose in Ben's throat. Even if they were all right for now, they wouldn't be able to stay much longer no matter how happy Charity was. He patted her hand, unable to reply.

Red Eagle leaned across the table. "Only Gabriel Dumont lives here. The others say they must go to their own families in St. Laurent and Batoche."

Ben frowned. This Red Eagle was full of surprises. First English, then French. He was right, though. Dumont's companions departed with hugs for Tante Madeleine and shouts of "*Au revoir*" fading into the growing twilight. Closing the door, Dumont turned to look across the room at the occupants of the table.

After a moment, he said, "*Bonsoir*, my friend Red Eagle. And who are these you have brought to my house—a young man and a princess?"

Red Eagle waited as Tante Madeleine spoke to her husband quietly in rapid French. Ben heard *malade* and knew she was explaining that Charity had been ill. But when she mentioned Uncle Lawrence, Dumont raised his eyebrows and laughed. Ben resented the laugh. His uncle was an important person—probably the most important in the district. Not only was he chief factor at Fort Carlton, but he was justice of the peace for the entire area. Unbidden, the words Uncle Lawrence had spoken that morning echoed in his head, and uneasiness overwhelmed him once more.

When Tante Madeleine turned to the black pot hanging in the fireplace, Dumont slipped off his boots and padded to the table. Some of Ben's concern faded as the man slid beside Red Eagle on the opposite bench, his grin open and friendly. He reached across the table to take Charity's hand with awkward gentleness. "Had I but known," he said, "my Madeleine had found a beautiful daughter to keep her happy while I was away, I would not have been concerned she may be lonely." He glanced at Ben. "And a son to help with the work."

Ben didn't know how to respond. Conditioned by his Irish father to feel superior to the Métis as well as to the Indians, he was confused. The man across from him held his head proudly, and the set of his powerful shoulders exuded strength. The ruggedness of his face was softened by the good humour in the wide grin, but the man's eyes were what Ben noticed most. They were warm and dark brown and gleamed with intelligence.

Remembering some of the manners his mother had tried to teach him, Ben stammered, "I...we...my sister and me—we're grateful. Madame Dumont kindly took us in and made Charity well. She came near to dying, I think, with a high fever. We'll leave before much longer."

Beside Ben, Charity caught her breath, and Madeleine Dumont's serene face was marred by a frown as she placed a tin plate overflowing with potage in front of her husband.

"Ben," she scolded, "you must think of your sister. Would you have her return to the fort still weak from fever? The damp and the woodsmoke there will bring on the cough again. Of that I am certain."

Dumont's head had been bent over his plate, and he raised it now to grin at Ben. "When Madame Dumont speaks as a healer, no one dares dispute her." His eyes on Charity, he added, "She brightens our home."

Tante Madeleine quickly added, "And you, as well, Ben. It has been good to have strong young hands to aid with the harvest."

"You live at Fort Carlton," Dumont said. "How is that?"

To spare Charity painful memories, Ben, briefly as possible, explained that his family had a small farm on the Red River and more than two years ago his father had taken off with some friends to hunt gold far in the west, leaving Ben and Charity with their mother to manage the farm. A year later their mother had died of the grippe, and her brother, Lawrence Clarke, had come to take charge. Ben felt his teeth clench as they always did when he remembered the black day a month after they buried his mother when Uncle Lawrence arrived and told him to pack their belongings. Since nobody had heard from Ben's father for two years, they likely never would, Uncle Lawrence had said, so he sold the stock and rented out the farm. He wanted to sell it, too, but Ben's father had to be away five years before the law would declare him legally dead.

"My pa will be back soon," Ben said for Charity's benefit. "And even if he isn't, next summer, soon as I'm sixteen, I'll take the farm back. We'll live on it same as we wanted to after our ma died instead of having to move to the fort." Lest he seem ungrateful, Ben added, "Uncle Lawrence did his best to help. He put the money from the stock in an account for us and got me a job at the fort to pay our keep there."

Dumont cocked an eyebrow as he regarded Ben. "I understand you have more than earned your keep here. I have need of a lad like you. You have observed the house I build for Madeleine?"

Ben nodded, and Dumont continued. "It will be big—bigger than Letendre's at Batoche. I have said it would be ready for her in the summer of next year, and with your help I will keep the promise." He leaned across the table to whisper to Charity, "Each day we will wipe your face with flour to make you pale and convince your brother you are sick. Thus we can keep you forever."

Charity giggled, but her brother couldn't smile. All Ben could think of was the look of cunning on Uncle Lawrence's face when he outlined his demands.

TWO

In the morning Red Eagle reported his horse was favouring one leg. After a quick examination, Dumont was able to dispel his fears. "It is nothing. He is old, that one, and the deer was a formidable burden. I will give you one of my beasts to ride and another to carry your meat. Ben will ride with you and return with the horses in the morning."

Ben had plenty of doubts about this arrangement. Rumours of unrest among treaty Indians had increased in the past year, and a night in their camp might be a bit uncomfortable.

When Dumont spoke again, Ben wondered if he could read minds. "Do not be concerned, young Ben," he said as he slipped a halter over the head of a chestnut-brown mare. "Poundmaker's people do not look for the scalp of a white man. Since the buffalo are no more, their thoughts are only with finding food for their children."

Ben flushed, and he avoided Red Eagle's eyes as he said, "There have to be some buffalo left somewheres. Just a few years back my pa told us he saw a herd so big it would take all day to ride through."

Dumont's eyes held a faraway look. "I remember well the days of the big hunt with the prairies black with herds."

Red Eagle looked over the back of the horse he was saddling. "Some say the Sioux and maybe the Blackfoot burn the grass along the border to keep the buffalo from drifting up here. Poundmaker says it is a lie of the white man, for the Sioux and Blackfoot starve, as well."

"Where'd they all go then?" Ben asked.

Dumont spread his hands in a gesture of helplessness. "We ask—"

The hammer of hoof beats interrupted the big man's words, and they all shaded their eyes against the morning sun. A large horse galloped toward them with a small boy on its back clutching the saddlehorn as he bounced. He called out, "Gabriel, Gabriel Dumont! You are wanted!"

"Ho, there young Vanda," Dumont said, frowning as the horse slid to a stop beside him. "Such a way to treat a friend? He has sweat dripping from all sides."

The boy gasped for breath as though his own legs had galloped across the prairie. "Monsieur, Papa said to fetch you at once. A man of great importance waits to speak to you."

Dumont slowly rubbed the chin under his beard as he regarded the excited child. "So? And how does the important man call himself?"

"I do not know. Bishop Grandin brought him. He wishes to see you."

Dumont raised bushy eyebrows. "So, if this great man is of sufficient importance for the bishop to travel so far from the comforts of St. Albert, surely I must hurry to meet with him." He turned to Red Eagle. "Vanda's farm is only a mile from here. We go together to hear this great man. If his words are of equal importance, I may go with you to meet again with Poundmaker."

Ben's heart began to beat faster. Maybe something was about to happen just as Uncle Lawrence had said, but Dumont's voice interrupted his thoughts. "And you, young Ben, will come with us."

The Vanda cabin was smaller than Dumont's and crowded with six Métis men standing along one wall and several children, who were quickly shooed outside when Dumont arrived. Ben recognized two of the men. One was big, happy Isidore Dumont, brother of Gabriel, and the other, a lean, sandy-haired fellow with blue eyes, who twice had stopped at the cabin to talk to Tante Madeleine before he used the ferry to cross the river. Ben knew him simply as Henry, the freighter.

In the centre of the room beside a wooden table covered with a fine white cloth sat a portly silver-haired man wearing a plain black cassock. Across from him a younger man appeared out of place in his heavy dark coat and vest with a wide white collar rising stiffly above a neatly tied cravat. Shiny black boots covered his legs. He rose to greet Dumont with a warm smile.

"Monsieur Dumont, it is an honour to meet at last the famous leader of the Métis. I am Amédée Forget, secretary to Lieutenant Governor Dewdney. He has sent me to speak with you on his behalf."

Ben was impressed. Lieutenant Governor Dewdney governed the whole North-West Territories.

Dumont approached Bishop Grandin and bent to kiss his ring before he nodded to Forget. "I am honoured, as well. But perhaps you will be disappointed to learn I am neither famous nor leader of all the Métis."

"But you are far too modest," Forget protested. "Wherever I go, I am told I must ask Gabriel Dumont, the chief."

Dumont shrugged. "It is true I was elected chief, but that was many years ago and then only to lead the great buffalo hunts. But they know I will always do what I can for the Métis, and for the Indians who are our blood brothers."

A small silence followed, broken when Forget demanded, "Then why in the spring did you travel to Montana and return with Louis Riel, a man who will surely bring only trouble to your people?"

A small smile lifted one corner of Dumont's mouth, and his words sharpened Ben's attention. "It seems those in Winnipeg or Ottawa must at last be giving attention to the telegrams sent by Lawrence Clarke."

For a brief moment a glint of humour warmed Forget's eyes. "The last one would have ended in the wastebasket with the others had not Riel's name caught my eye. You must admit he is a troublemaker."

"I agree, but Clarke is only doing what he believes to be right to protect the interests of the Hudson's Bay Company, so we are able to forgive him."

For a moment Forget looked very young as he struggled with his confusion. Then his face cleared, and he frowned. "Monsieur Dumont, you toy with me. You know full well I speak of Riel as a troublemaker, not Clarke. I must repeat—why did you travel to Montana and bring back Riel and his family?"

Dumont sighed. "I am a simple man and leave it to those who are well educated to debate our cause, but I do not have to be well schooled to know the government of Canada cares little for the Métis, or the Indians. We try to be both fair and patient, but the fine John Macdonald bothers not to answer the petitions we send."

"This Riel is not the answer to your problems," Forget said.

"Fifteen years ago on the Red River, Louis Riel found a way to get the attention of the government," Dumont said, "and it seems he has done the same for us now, for you have come at last to talk, have you not?"

Bishop Grandin appeared troubled as he interrupted. "My son," he said to Dumont, "you know Riel, at the time of which you speak, became so carried away with his perceived power that he caused a man to be shot and had to flee to Montana. And now we hear he suggests he is more powerful than our pope. Think carefully. Is this the man you wish to represent you?"

Dumont murmured a reply to the bishop, then turned to hear Forget ask, "What is this petition you say was ignored?"

"More than one. Many more." Holding up a callused hand, Dumont ticked off his fingers as he spoke. "Seven years ago, from St. Laurent to Battleford on both branches of the Saskatchewan River, petitions were sent to ask that land claims be settled. The buffalo are gone, and now we must depend on farming and wood-cutting and, if we are fortunate, some freighting. Our land is everything to us, and we wish to be protected from swindlers such as those who took Métis land in Manitoba. Also, you granted Métis land to the Hudson's Bay Company and the railway, the rest to be sold by the government except for that allowed for homesteading. A piece here, a parcel there, without regard for those who settled here long ago."

Forget broke in smoothly. "But I understand you have no need for concern. Your land is one of the parcels allotted for homesteading and you have fulfilled the requirements, so you will be allowed to keep it."

Dumont nodded. "True, I am one of the fortunate, but others—Métis, whites, and mixed bloods—who have farmed their land as long as I, now must leave because Canada has decreed they are not on homestead land. This is not to be endured."

Forget took a deep breath. "Many times it has been explained to the Métis and all others who settled along the rivers here that this was Dominion land, surveyed by the government at great cost so it could be settled in an orderly fashion. This was done long before most of these people arrived and squatted on land to which they had no right. Now they want a survey again to suit the shape of the land they took so they can claim it as their homesteads."

"The shape of the land is of great importance if each is to

have use of the river. We ask only the lots be on the river with small frontage and extend back to the woods and those who have been on their land three years be granted rights to that land. All others must be given land scrip—enough to buy a quarter section so they may settle elsewhere."

"You must admit," Bishop Grandin said to Forget, "that is not an unreasonable request."

"There is more," Dumont said. "We have much concern for our blood brothers—the Cree and the Assiniboine—who received fine promises when they agreed to go to reserves. Do those in Ottawa care that they are starving and cold?"

"Perhaps those who care have trouble finding money to help the reserves," Forget said. "Times are hard for everyone in Canada right now. However, promises must be kept. I will do my best. Anything else?"

Dumont reached inside his buckskin tunic and brought out a folded paper. "It was written at our last meeting," he said, handing it to Forget. "We will obey your laws only when we also have the rights that all others have in Canada."

Forget's tone was light. "I am sure you do not mean that as a threat."

Dumont was leaning on the door, his thumbs hooked in the wide red sash around his waist. He straightened now, and as he reached for the door latch, he looked at each of the other six Métis in the room before he turned back to Forget and said, "You have the message on the paper. But for me, add this—the Métis are more than a nation of those who lead and those who follow. We are one family and regard the whites and English-speaking mixed bloods beside our rivers as our cousins. If one should lose his land, all would feel the loss. And the suffering on the reserves is our suffering, as well."

Forget said nothing. Instead, he pulled on his bottom lip thoughtfully as he regarded the Métis leader.

Dumont finally said, "*Au revoir*, Your Grace, Monsieur Forget."

Ben was the first to follow through the doorway, and he stood beside Dumont as the rest of the Métis men crowded around him, speaking in low voices. His good humour apparently restored, Dumont raised a hand and smiled. "It is a forward step, this meeting with Forget. Now they listen. Some of you must ride to Batoche to report to Riel and the others. Caution them. Tell them now is the time for patience. As for me, I will see Poundmaker. Perhaps Forget will keep his word and there will be more food for the Cree this winter."

Ben's thoughts raced even as he struggled to understand the rapidly spoken French. He knew with sickening certainty that this was the kind of thing his uncle wanted him to report. Then Dumont called to Ben, and relief washed over him as he realized that even if he wanted to, he couldn't rush over to Fort Carlton and tell his uncle everything. He had to ride with Red Eagle and bring back the horses. Maybe by the time he saw his uncle again, everybody at Fort Carlton would know about the meeting with the government man. It likely wasn't meant to be kept secret.

Dumont interrupted his thoughts again. "Mount up, my young friends. It is time we carry the deer back to the camp."

Just for today Ben decided to put aside his worries and enjoy the ride. Fall was his favourite time of year—always had been, even when it meant there would be lessons to do again. He understood why Charity looked forward to school each year; she had a love of learning. But for him, figuring out the parts of speech in a sentence couldn't compare with the sweet smell of hay when stacked, or the bright gold and red of leaves that meant grain should be put in the barn and potatoes stored in the root cellar. And then there would be his mother canning sweet corn, tomatoes, and saskatoon berries for winter pies. It was hard work, but when it was done there was plenty to last until spring. To his horror, Ben realized his eyes smarted and, worse, Gabriel Dumont was looking at him.

"Ben," the big man said, "as I gave my farewell, Charity asked if we might pass by Fort Carlton. She would not reveal to me why she asks this, but I am concerned. Is it possible she now longs for the family of your uncle?"

Ben shook his head. "Last year Uncle Lawrence sent his family to Prince Albert to live. It's her books she wants. I was there two days ago and meant to bring some, but I forgot."

Dumont smiled broadly. "*Bien*. The problem is small. But I find it strange that—"

"That she wants her books when she can't see?"

Red Eagle, who was riding ahead, dropped back to listen.

"Yes," Dumont said. "But I do not wish to intrude."

Ben swallowed hard. "Charity used to be able to see. We lived back east, and I guess we were about three when Pa decided to come west to farm. Our mother liked books and she brought all we had. When we were twelve, Charity had a fever that made her blind. After that we quit riding off to school at the Red River settlement, and our mother used the books to teach me reading and sums. Most of the books are fixed in Charity's memory. She'd read them that much before she got blind. I been reading the rest to her."

"Charity wishes to have the books with pictures to show the young ones when she tells the story," Red Eagle said.

Ben's head snapped up, and he frowned. "How'd you know that?"

"While you slept, she spoke to me of this as we took the horses to the river to drink."

Charity was too friendly by half, Ben thought darkly. She was like their mother, who had always tried to convince their father that there was good in all kinds of people.

Dumont waved an arm skyward. "So it is settled. We must get the books for Mademoiselle Charity when we return."

They travelled steadily, but by the time they reached the waiting hunters, the sun had slipped behind the hills humped along the river. As they halted their mounts, one of the men by the fire rose. Without being told, Ben knew this was Poundmaker, and he wondered foolishly if the Hudson's Bay Company ever stocked britches long enough to cover someone so tall. Although Dumont himself stood more than six feet, the Indian towered above him. But he was much thinner than the Métis. Under a worn brown shirt the bones of his massive shoulders stood out like knobs on a dresser drawer, and beneath each cheekbone a hollow lay in the long, flat planes of his face. His eyes, sunken and dark, held a look of sadness, but below the straight nose a generous mouth looked as though it was accustomed to smiling.

Realizing he was staring, Ben slid from his horse and stood beside it while Dumont and Red Eagle greeted the men. To discourage predators, the deer was raised high with a short rope of braided deerskin snaked over a limb of a half-grown cottonwood not far from the campfire. In the growing twilight Ben noted carcasses hanging from another tree—seven in all. There would be a big welcome for the men when they got back to their reserve.

There was little more talk until the horses were staked out to graze on a patch of meadow. When they returned to the fire, Ben saw the strips of meat on a stick above the coals, and his stomach growled. Although hungry enough to eat his saddle, it didn't seem right to take food meant for people who never had enough. Red Eagle dropped to sit cross-legged by the fire. Without looking up, he said, "Eat. The hunt has been good. There is enough."

Dumont nudged Ben. "You would not want to offend, my son. They wish to share. And I have bannock and tea sent by my lady to go with the meat."

His saddle might have been easier to chew, Ben reflected, but he didn't care. Nothing had ever tasted better, though he took barely enough to satisfy his hunger. When they finished, Dumont and the hunters fell into a deep discussion, but since they spoke in Cree and Red Eagle wasn't bothering to interpret for his benefit, Ben decided to find a spot for his bedroll. He rose and quietly announced his intention to Red Eagle. Knowing he would be covered with flies by morning if he didn't wash the smell of deer meat from his face and hands, he added, "Think I'll go down to the river first."

Their camp was perched on a steep bluff over the river, and Ben had to walk a short distance upstream until he came to a narrow game trail leading down through the waist-high brush to the water. Halfway down, he paused to survey the effect created by the slowly rising fat white moon. A dozen yards upstream a jumble of rocks given up by a cataclysm long ago stretched across the water to form a small, lustily roaring waterfall. The spray thrown up in the moonlight equalled the lights of a million tiny lanterns.

Taking in the beauty of the night, Ben vowed to remember it all so he could describe it to Charity. From the corner of his eye, as he gazed downward, he saw a flash of silver shoot from the river beyond the cascade. It dropped back before he could be certain, but it had to be a fish. And what a fish!

Excited, Ben half slid down the trail and followed it as it wound upstream to end not far above the rocks. He tried not to take his eyes from the spot where the fish had surfaced, but when it leaped again it was several yards upstream and bigger than ever. His pulse raced as he pushed through the willows and fumbled in his coat pocket for the line and hook he always carried. He couldn't tell what kind of fish it was, but a couple like that would be enough breakfast for everybody.

Kneeling, Ben rubbed his fingers in the soft, damp earth along the edge of the water until he felt the hard shell of a beetle to bait his hook The wriggling silver body of the fish shot in the air almost directly opposite him, but Ben's heart sank; it was half across the river—too far to cast his line. Maybe not, though. His searching eyes located a wide bulge in the river bottom about ten feet from shore. Unless the moonlight deceived, it appeared the water couldn't be more than a foot deep over the bar. A pair of good jumps and he would be a lot closer to where the fish played. Hastily Ben stood on one foot, then the other, to pull off his boots before he rolled up his pant legs.

His first leap carried him into ankle-deep sand covered by water up to his knees. Another carried him to the sandbar. One more and he would be in the middle of the river. He tried to lift his foot, but it was held fast. His knees began to sink through the water into oozing, shifting sand.

THREE

Instinctively Ben tried to twist his body. He might be able to reach an overhanging branch from a willow bush on the shore. With the effort, he sank deeper into the mire. Halfway to his hips now, he knew further struggle would be worse than useless. He filled his lungs and shouted, "Hallooo!" When there was no answering cry, his heart sank. Maybe they had all gone to sleep. "Hallooo!" he called again and again. With sudden despair he remembered the roar of the water rushing over the rocks downstream. "They can't hear me," he said, his lips forming the words without sound. "Who's to look after Charity? Oh, Ma, I'm sorry." Just then he heard a rustling, no louder than the soft gurgle of the rippling water, and knew he wasn't alone. "Ma? Is that you, Ma?"

"No, but perhaps she is the one who told me to come," a voice said from the riverbank. "Be very still, Ben."

"Red Eagle! Get a rope!"

"There is no time. You must do as I say. Fall back as far as you can on the water and stretch your arms to me. I will throw one end of my coat to you."

"I'm too far. Stay out. Even close to shore you'd get stuck, too. I felt it shift there."

"Do as I say. Now!"

Ben threw himself backward and felt his bottom sink in the sand. But as his head and shoulders slid under the water, his torso straightened and he flung his arms over his head. Water flowed across his face, and something touched his fingertips. He stretched his arms to grasp it, but it was no use. He lifted his head to gasp for breath and felt sand creep across his stomach.

"You are right," Red Eagle muttered. "I must find—" He was silent for a moment before he said, "Now, Ben, again."

Water flooded into Ben's ears and eyes, and he didn't hear the other boy slip onto the river's surface. However, he felt the grip on the middle of his arms and, in turn, he grasped Red Eagle's forearms. He felt an upward movement and lifted his head.

"Breathe deep," Red Eagle commanded, "and pull."

After filling his lungs, Ben lay back in the water. With arms locked together, they pitted their strength against the sucking sand. An inch at a time Ben's knees slipped upward, and three times Red Eagle signalled for him to lift his head to gulp air before the muck released its grip.

"I will let go now," Red Eagle said, "but do not move."

Unable to see what the other was doing, Ben half floated, arms stretched over his head, and forced himself not to wonder how it would feel if his entire length dropped through the shallow water into the waiting sand.

"Catch," Red Eagle commanded. Ben's fingers clutched one sleeve of the coat that touched his waiting hands. "Hold it and roll over. I can pull you now."

A moment later both boys flopped to the ground at the

water's edge, breathing hard. Ben shuddered. The skin on his legs felt gritty and his wet shirt was icy against his skin. He looked around for the coat he had dropped before he had jumped into the water and found it tied around the base of a sturdy willow bush. "So that's how you did it," he said, gesturing to the coat. "You hooked your feet between the coat and the bush and spread yourself flat on the water."

Red Eagle shrugged. "There was no other way."

"And you used your coat to pull me out."

"It is nothing."

There was an embarrassed silence as they regarded each other. Ben struggled for the right words to tell Red Eagle he was grateful. The Cree could have run for help instead of taking a chance on getting stuck himself. Painfully Ben realized what a fool he was for thinking he was better than Red Eagle. Disgust rolled through him in waves. How could he tell this boy that he wished he had been more friendly these past two days? Now, most likely, it was too late. He wanted to tell Red Eagle a pile of things, but all he could do was mumble, "Thanks. I owe you. I owe you a whole lot."

"It is nothing," Red Eagle repeated. "Would you not do the same?"

Ben made a startling discovery: something in Red Eagle's voice said he felt uncomfortable, too. They were really much the same, Ben told himself, feeling strange. He knew that even if they were similar in most ways, in others they were quite different. Yet underneath he was sure they both wanted to be friends but were afraid of making fools of themselves if the other one didn't feel likewise. Ben now knew what to say, and he grinned. "Sure, I would, but first I'd make you say please."

Gabriel Dumont's voice cut through their laughter, and they looked up to see his bulky outline on the brow of the hill above them, fists on hips. "It is a cause for humour to sit in the night air in wet shirts?"

Ben explained. “I fell in quicksand, and Red Eagle pulled me out.”

“So? And how does one just fall into quicksand?”

Ben had forgotten the fish. He turned to Red Eagle. “It was the fish, Red Eagle. It was the biggest fish I ever saw, and I had to get out a ways to hook him for our breakfast.”

“Leave this fish for another day,” Dumont suggested, “and come dry yourself. If you return to Madame Dumont with aching head and fever, she will have my ears.”

Later, wrapped in Poundmaker’s blanket and seated by the campfire, Ben was encouraged by the chief to relate his adventure in detail while Dumont interpreted his words. It was strangely satisfying to be the centre of attention among these stern-faced hunters as he described how Red Eagle had lain on his stomach in the water to pull him free. He made certain they understood the danger for his friend.

Not long after, rolled up in his blanket, Ben lay on his back close to the fire where it had warmed the earth. The blanket was all he had between the ground and his bare skin, causing him to shiver. His clothes steamed on a tripod over the coals. Although bone-tired, he found sleep elusive; he was too exhilarated. Not only had he made a friend, it was plain he had been accepted by these men, especially Poundmaker. Ben smiled in the dark as he recalled how good it had been to sit by the fire and listen to their stories of great hunts and battles while Red Eagle murmured steadily beside him to explain their words and gestures.

Ben stared up at the sky and thought again about his rescue from the river. Across the fire, Dumont snored lustily, but no sound came from Red Eagle nearby. Maybe, Ben thought, he was still awake. “Psst, you sleeping?” he whispered.

“Of course. What else should I be doing?”

Ben grinned but quickly grew serious. The stars above reminded him of what Red Eagle had said when he found him in the river—it might have been his mother who had told the

Cree to come. It was the kind of thing that might be all right for Charity to think about, but more than anything, he didn't want his new friend to get the idea he was given to having fanciful thoughts like a girl. Maybe he could sidle up to his question. He turned his head and whispered, "Uh, I was wondering...you never said how it was you happened to come upriver and find me stuck in the mud."

Red Eagle was silent for so long that Ben thought he might have gone to sleep. When the Cree did reply, he, too, was hesitant. "Ben, I would like to say I heard the voice of your mother tell me you needed help, but it would not be true. You were away a long time for only washing your hands, and I knew the direction you had taken. Remember, I said to you in the forest that you make noise equal to a bear."

Ben didn't know what he had expected Red Eagle to say, but before he could think of a reply, the Indian added, "But it is also true that I do not know why I stopped listening to the talk around the fire and wondered where you were."

A light touch of frost had sparkled over the prairie, but before they waved farewell to Poundmaker, the morning sun wiped it away and left the stems of sagebrush and clumps of grass damp and pungent. They rode in companionable silence, Ben in the middle between Dumont and Red Eagle, for it had been decided the Cree boy would return to Gabriel's Crossing to become the messenger between there and Poundmaker's reserve. Ben was delighted. Maybe Red Eagle would be at the Crossing all winter.

With that thought his heart skipped a beat. It was uncertain how long he and Charity would live at Gabriel's Crossing. Uncle Lawrence had said Ben had only a few days to agree to his plan. Then, too, for all Tante Madeleine's generosity, it was a serious undertaking to feed two extra mouths, though Charity ate little and he could cut down himself. But now there was Red Eagle, too. It occurred to Ben that people weren't much different from wild animals—their whole life aimed at finding enough to eat and a place to keep warm. Maybe he could help somehow.

Ben broke the silence. "Monsieur Dumont—" he began.

"Here, we are not so formal. Gabriel will do."

Ben grinned and started again. "I know game's scarce, but maybe we should keep a sharp eye for rabbits or maybe a deer."

"That we will do, but the hunting is best downriver from St. Laurent. Do not be concerned, for tomorrow we will slaughter one of the cattle. As well, with two young men to hunt with him, Gabriel Dumont will have enough to feed all of Batoche before ice covers the river."

Red Eagle and Ben looked at each other. Not for nothing did some of the Métis refer to Dumont as a lion; two months of stalking game with the prairies' greatest hunter was a thing for a boy to dream about. As quickly as it had come, Ben's grin disappeared and his shoulders slumped. There would be more to staying at the Dumont cabin than hunting and fishing. For a moment he had forgotten about his uncle and what else he was supposed to do.

A hand touched his arm, and he glanced over to see Red Eagle's questioning frown. "There is something wrong?"

Ben forced a smile. "No, it just hurts my head when I think hard, that's all."

"And what is it that causes your head to work so hard?" Dumont asked.

Needing a safe subject, Ben said, "I was thinking about Poundmaker. It surprised me when I saw him. He's a sight younger than I expected." Ben decided it might not be a good idea to mention he was even more surprised by Poundmaker's intelligence and dry sense of humour.

Dumont thought for a moment, then said, "Only a man who is a great hunter or great warrior or has shown great wisdom can be made a chief of his band. Poundmaker is respected by all the bands. Among each of the great nations there is always one with much influence. Crowfoot is such a one for the Blackfoot, Sitting Bull for the Sioux. It is so for Poundmaker with the Cree."

In the late afternoon they paused to let their horses drink from a small feeder stream. "Five miles ahead is the trail to Fort Carlton," Dumont said, his eyes moving from one boy to the other. "Here we part. I return to the Crossing, and you take the packhorse to the fort to fetch these things for Charity. We will expect you by midday tomorrow."

The small hope his uncle wouldn't be at the fort disappeared as Ben, followed by Red Eagle, rode through the gates and saw the skinny, stooped figure of Lawrence Clarke emerge from the trade room. A short, dark man, clean-shaven except for a thick, drooping moustache, followed him. Ben recognized the second man as Chief Trader Thomas McKay. His uncle looked up as Ben dismounted, and with a brief word to McKay, hurried forward, his thin lips stretched in a smile.

"Well, Ben, I didn't think I'd see you again so soon." With a glance at Red Eagle, Clarke's smile disappeared. "Why did you bring him?"

"He saved me from the river," Ben said. "We were off somewhere with Gabriel Dumont, and I saw a fish to catch. Red Eagle saved—" He stopped himself, realizing he had said too much. The mere mention of the Métis's name had sparked interest in his uncle's eyes.

"Come," the chief factor said, taking Ben's arm. "After we have supper, we'll talk." When two Hudson's Bay clerks came out of the trade room and greeted Ben, Clarke told them, "Show the Indian where to put the horses and see he gets something to eat."

Ben dug in his heels and started to protest, but Red Eagle shook his head. Uneasily Ben went with his uncle to the big house, the chief factor's residence when he was in the fort. As Ben took his place at the table, he searched for words to make his uncle understand why he couldn't do what had been asked of him. He knew saying them wouldn't be easy.

Before he could muster the courage, his uncle leaned over and whispered, "I have information for you to take back to the Métis that might cause some of those rebellious scoundrels to think twice before they make unreasonable demands on the Dominion." Nodding in the direction of the chief trader and a half-dozen men who joined them at the long table, he said, "We'll talk in my office when we finish. Though McKay is Métis, he's loyal to the company. But two of the clerks might be more inclined to sympathize with the rebels." Clarke straightened, then raised his voice. "Now, perhaps you'll tell us how the Indian saved your life."

Every eye turned in Ben's direction, and though he was uncomfortable with the attention, he told his story briefly without mentioning either Gabriel Dumont or Poundmaker. There was a murmur of approval for Red Eagle when Ben finished, which encouraged him to say, "I think I have some funds in my account for clerking here and thought I'd draw on them to buy a gift for Red Eagle."

Ben had a pretty good idea what his uncle was thinking as the man's scowl was replaced by a thin smile. He had gambled that Uncle Lawrence wouldn't want the listening men to know his nephew hadn't been paid for work done in the fort, and he was right.

"Of course," his uncle finally said. "See Mr. McKay in the morning."

Even though most of the land around Fort Carlton was too swampy for farming, there was no shortage of food at this table; the days of pemmican as a staple diet and buffalo nose as a delicacy were past. Beef and pork came by river aboard paddle wheelers and by wagon on the Carlton Trail from the Red River farmers as well as from those closer at hand along the Saskatchewan River. There were apples, too, and Ben decided to take some when he left. They could eat the fruit and plant the seeds on the edge of Tante Madeleine's garden.

The talk around the table reflected Uncle Lawrence's prediction of an imminent uprising. It seemed not only the French-speaking Métis and the Indians upset him, but also those descended from Indian mothers and British men whom he referred to as "English-speaking Métis" and the "whites" who had a man from Prince Albert named William Henry Jackson for their spokesman.

"Jackson could get thick as thieves with Riel, but an alliance of Métis and whites wouldn't last long," his uncle said darkly. "The whites want one thing only—title to the land they claim they homesteaded and lower rates for their grain shipments. They have little concern for the Métis, and less for the Indians."

The meal was over too quickly for Ben, and the moment he dreaded arrived when his uncle took his arm and propelled him down a narrow hallway to the office, with McKay following. The two older men seated themselves on polished wooden chairs with padded seats near the straight-legged table that served as a desk. Ben sat on a bench against a wall.

His uncle placed his hands on the table and peered at Ben with a look of anticipation. "Now then, tell me what you've learned."

Goose bumps popped out on Ben's arms as he looked back at the two men and tried to explain that he had come to the fort only to get Charity's books and some of his belongings.

"Come, come, Ben," his uncle coaxed. "Don't hesitate because Mr. McKay is here. He's as eager as I am to keep the North-West Territories free from warfare and is as grateful as I am to know you're a loyal subject of Queen Victoria."

Ben fastened on one of the thoughts that had darted in and out of his head while dining. Maybe he did have information that might appease his uncle for now, news the whole fort would hear about sooner or later. He cleared his throat and told the two men that Lieutenant Governor Dewdney had sent

Amédée Forget, his secretary, to meet with the Métis.

"We already got word from Winnipeg that Forget would do just that," McKay said.

"Nothing more?" his uncle, plainly disappointed, asked. "But what about Gabriel Dumont? Where did you go with him?"

"Red Eagle shot a deer, but his horse was too lame to carry it, so we took a packhorse and rode back to his hunting camp with him."

"And after that?"

Ben wet his lips. "We camped for the night with the other hunters and started back this morning. "We—Red Eagle and me—split off and came here to get some of the things Charity left."

Clarke took a deep breath. "I see. And I suppose you don't know what was discussed with the Indians."

Ben shook his head. "They talked in Cree."

McKay was watching Ben with narrowed eyes. "Being raised a Métis myself, I know how friendly they can be and generous, too, but they're too easily led into trouble. Make no mistake, Ben, they're getting some bad advice from Riel, and it's up to people like us and you to see they don't do something foolish."

Ben's thoughts were confused. Put like that, maybe what he was doing wasn't really spying. But how could he judge what was good for the Métis and what wasn't? He needed time to think, and to talk to Charity.

In the morning Ben and Red Eagle grinned at each other as they rode out of the fort. Ben felt good. Before they met to load up in the morning, he had gone to the trade room with McKay. He figured the chief trader had been more than fair in totalling up the pay he had coming, for there was plenty of money to buy a shiny new Winchester rifle for Red Eagle and gifts for Tante Madeleine and Dumont. Ben wanted to be prepared if they were fortunate enough to be in the Dumont house for Christmas and the New Year celebrations. He had gifts to hide until then, but for now he had spices and corn syrup for Tante Madeleine. And, not knowing if she was low on her supply of sugar, he had bought a sack of it. For Dumont there was a large tin of fine English tea and a good supply of shells for the hunting rifle he referred to as Le Petit. The books alone would be enough to gladden Charity's heart, but he hadn't been able to resist the stock of maple syrup bars from Quebec. She had a weakness for candy.

Looking forward to giving his presents, Ben tried to ignore the sense of impending disaster kicking up a storm in his stomach. The message his uncle had said to pass on was: Lieutenant Governor Dewdney had promised by January 1 that an army of North-West Mounted Police would be in Fort Carlton to keep the peace.

FOUR

September passed more swiftly than Ben could ever remember, for there was much work to be done before winter, and most of it fell to Red Eagle and him. Although Dumont only shrugged when Ben relayed Lawrence Clarke's information about the police, he was often away at meetings in Batoche and St. Laurent. When he returned, he never failed to be generous with his praise for the work the two boys had done.

Ben and Red Eagle spent more than a week shoring up the walls inside the root cellar and lining the entrance with mounds of hay so the frost in the winter air wouldn't rush in each time the door was opened. After that they piled the roof deeply with manure hauled from the barn, so the potatoes, pumpkins, carrots, cabbages, and corn could be shielded from the penetrating cold that would otherwise drift downward and inside. When they finished, Ben turned to Red Eagle and blurted a question that had been on his mind as they worked. "How is it we grow enough here to last the winter and your people go hungry?"

He was relieved to see Red Eagle wasn't offended, and there was only patience in his tone as he explained. "Ben, here we are five. In my village there are more than two hundred stomachs to fill, but we have little more land than Gabriel for growing food. Much of our reserve is covered with big rocks and there is swampland. Also, when too much rain washes away the seeds, or burrowing animals eat the first shoots, we have no more to plant. Here one can borrow from a neighbour or find more in a store." He smiled, but there was no hope in his voice. "Perhaps in time."

Even Charity had work to do for the coming winter. Dumont's face had reflected his pride as he pointed out a round metal tub with a lid on top and a wooden treadle on the bottom that sat beside the cabin. "It is the only washing machine west of Winnipeg, and it belongs to the wife of Gabriel Dumont."

Charity spent her mornings in the shade of a yellowing cottonwood singing to herself as first one foot, then the other worked the treadle up and down while the paddle in the machine swished the clothes back and forth in the hot, soapy water. After three verses of "Two Little Birds with Pointed Beaks" and two of "In the Morning When I Get Up," she stopped. Then, with the aid of a forked stick, she hauled out the garments one at a time and dumped them in a nearby tub of cold water to plunge them up and down with her hands. Twisting them hard to wring out the water, she plopped them in a basket for Tante Madeleine to hang to dry.

After the second morning, Ben saw that Charity's hands were red and chapped, and he started to suggest he should be the one to wring out the wet clothes when he felt Tante Madeleine's fingers touch his lips. Beckoning, she walked a short distance before she turned to him. "Ben, I have salve to put on Charity's hands, but I have nothing to heal a hurt in her heart if she comes to believe she is without use."

Ben's throat tightened with gratitude as he looked at the serene face of the Métis woman. "Guess I never thought of that. I should've, though. I've never seen her any happier than she is right now."

That wasn't quite true. Charity had been happier here before he returned from Fort Carlton with her books—and with the ultimatum from Uncle Lawrence.

With Dumont and Red Eagle away on an errand in Batoche, and Tante Madeleine working in her garden, Ben had seized the opportunity to talk with his sister alone. When he finished telling Charity that Uncle Lawrence had demanded he spy on Dumont and his friends and watch Riel closely, she was shocked and angry with Ben for even considering such a thing.

"I know," Ben had agreed. "It makes me feel lower than a snake, but if I don't, it's certain he's going to make us go back to the fort."

Charity was silent for a long moment before she said, "Even so, Ben, you mustn't do anything that might hurt Gabriel or Tante Madeleine or any of these people. Promise you won't."

To make Charity happy again, he had agreed, even though he had promised himself he and Charity would never go back to Fort Carlton to live with their uncle.

The snows were sudden and heavy in November without bringing the cozy sense of isolation Ben had felt in the farmhouse on the Red River, for with the Métis, winter was a time to socialize. In spite of a strict upbringing that disapproved of dancing and card playing, Ben enjoyed everything. It was best in the long evenings when, ignoring the snow and cold, neighbouring families frequently dropped by for billiards in Dumont's little store near the ferry, or to play cards and tell stories in the house. Often Father André, with Father Moulin or Father Fourmond, tapped on the door, sometimes with a jug of their well-liked rhubarb wine. Tante Madeleine was delighted to see them, and Charity liked them, too. But Ben was uncomfortable, not because he wasn't a Catholic, but because the talk too often turned to politics and problems he preferred not to think about.

Once Henry, the freighter, had dropped in, and spent a week at Dumont's urging. Ben enjoyed Henry, for he had endless stories to tell of his adventures as he drove his freight wagon from the United States to the North-West Territories. Ben never learned where the man lived or from where he came. The only personal thing Henry said about himself was: "My pa's from Scotland and my ma was Assiniboine. I always figured that made me an improved Scotsman."

Twice they dressed in their finest clothing, bundled into blankets in the horse-drawn wagon, and travelled to a wedding in nearby Batoche. Charity loved the weddings, for there was music from violins, harmonicas, guitars, even drums. And if there were no instruments, spoons banging on bowls would do. With Red Eagle always at her side to make sure none of the whirling dancers crashed into her, she clapped in rhythm with the music. Near dawn Tante Madeleine would lead her to a pallet on the floor in an adjoining room set aside for the women and children. The boys and men made do with their bedrolls in the hayloft of the barn.

It was at the second of the two weddings, as Tante Madeline was trying to teach him to dance a reel, that Ben looked over her shoulder to the bench where his sister sat and got an unpleasant surprise. Smiling, Charity was tracing her fingertips slowly over Red Eagle's face. "Whoa now!" Ben muttered, unaware he had tightened his hold on Tante Madeleine's hand enough to crush her fingers.

When her eyes followed Ben's stare, Madeleine Dumont stopped dancing and led him aside. "Think before you speak, Ben. You may destroy forever what you hold dear."

Ben seemed not to hear as he moved toward his sister and Red Eagle. When Ben appeared at his side, the Cree glanced up and said, "Charity sees me."

At the sound of Red Eagle's words, Charity's hands dropped into her lap and her smile widened. "Is that Ben?" Without waiting for a reply, her face radiant, she said, "Oh, Ben, I've made a wonderful discovery. Now I know how Red Eagle looks, and I'm going to ask Tante Madeleine and Gabriel if they will allow me to feel their faces so I can see them in my head."

Ben felt a rush of embarrassed gratitude for whatever had made him hesitate before he scolded Charity for being familiar with Red Eagle. Now he grinned. "You should've asked me what he looks like. I could've told you how ugly he is." His humour came too late, though, for Red Eagle had seen Ben's angry face. The Cree stood up, watchful and silent.

"What is it?" Charity asked, sensing the sudden tension. "Red Eagle, you know Ben was only joking, don't you? I feel something...something..."

Tante Madeleine appeared at his side, and Ben was thankful for the interruption. With a movement of her head, she indicated Dumont, who stood with a group of men a few feet away. "The old lion would like to sleep in his own den tonight. We must leave now, for it is late."

Ben tried to join in the singing as they drove back to Gabriel's Crossing, but his heart wasn't in it. He knew Red Eagle was offended, and he didn't know how to make it right without embarrassing them both. When they reached the cabin, they climbed to their beds in the loft in silence. Ben lay in the dark, wide-eyed and worried as images of the past few months flitted into his mind: Red Eagle and he, finished with their day's work, chasing each other with pails of the water they should have used to wash themselves; Red Eagle patiently teaching him how to set a snare for rabbits; Red Eagle taking his turn with a book in front of the fire to read aloud to Charity. He thought of his friend's eyes the first time they had hunted downriver with Dumont and how the Cree had shot a buck cleanly with his new Winchester. Pondering all of this, Ben turned over in the dark and sighed noisily. For a few minutes he listened hopefully, half expecting Red Eagle would ask why he wasn't asleep, but there was only silence in the loft.

In the morning Ben awoke later than usual, opening his eyes to see flickering shadows on the beamed ceiling over his head cast by the warm light from the fireplace below. Yawning, he sniffed the pungent smell of dried fish liberally sprinkled with pepper the way Dumont liked it. As he scrambled to find his boots, he wondered what time it was. Red Eagle's bedroll was empty. He slid down the rough ladder and greeted Charity, who emerged from her curtained-off space at the end of the long room.

"Morning," he said. "I guess I slept late. Red Eagle's up and gone."

Tante Madeleine came from the kitchen. "Red Eagle went with Gabriel to feed the horses. They will be here soon for breakfast."

"I'll go help," Ben said, starting for the door, but the woman touched his shoulder.

"There is no need. Sit. You do more than your share, Ben, and they must be finished by now."

Dumont returned to the cabin alone. "Red Eagle is not hungry," he announced as he removed his heavy wool coat, "and sends word he will gather the eggs for you. It is my hope the feathers tickle his fingers enough to make him smile, for he is very solemn this morning."

Charity's expression was anxious. "Red Eagle isn't sick, is he, Gabriel? I don't believe he spoke once when we returned last night. He went right to bed."

Tante Madeleine spoke soothingly. “He is tired only. And who is not after two days of wedding celebration?” She reached for Charity’s hand. “Come, *chérie*, your porridge grows cold.”

Trying not to reveal his uneasiness, Ben piped up with, “Sure, that’s it. I’ll go talk to him.”

The top half of the door was open, and through it Ben saw Red Eagle staring out a small dusty window in the side of the barn. He whirled when the hinges on the bottom of the door announced Ben’s arrival.

Fumbling for some way to break the uneasiness between them, Ben asked, “Gathering eggs?” Jehoshaphat! he thought. That was brilliant.

Red Eagle gestured downward at the empty basket on the floor.

Unable to tolerate the silence, Ben blurted, “Look, Red Eagle, you got to understand…I…my looking ugly wasn’t because— I just thought…”

Red Eagle looked away, and his voice was so low Ben could scarcely hear the words. “You saw Charity touch my face. You thought she was showing me feelings of…of affection.”

“Come on, Red Eagle,” Ben almost shouted. Then he paused to think before he continued more quietly. “Sure, I guess you’re right in a way, but not like you think. It just hit me wrong at first, thinking she was, well, like you said, being affectionate. But not because it was you. I just never thought about Charity being old enough for that kind of stuff.”

“Charity is the same age you are.”

Ben nodded. “I know, and I guess I have to start thinking about what happens if someone wants to marry her someday.”

Red Eagle turned to the window again. “If we were in the time before the buffalo were no more, before we agreed to live on land chosen by white men, I would say to you I would guard Charity with my life. Among my people she would be a princess known for her beauty and gentle ways, and from the woods and across the prairies they would come to hear her stories.”

He shrugged his thin shoulders and looked directly at Ben. "But now you have no need to fear I would ever ask for Charity's hand and you would have to search for a way to refuse without giving me pain, for among my people there is only hunger and disease to offer her."

Ben's chest constricted, and his words were choked. "That was a fine thing you said, Red Eagle. And it relieves me a lot to know you feel that way, because now, if something happens to me and the Dumonts can't do it, I know you'll see to it that Charity gets someplace where she'll be safe."

"This I promise."

Ben stepped closer and put his hand on Red Eagle's shoulder. "Charity's proud, and I'm proud, too, to have you for a friend. If I live to be a hundred and fifteen, I'll never have a better."

With each passing day, Ben's understanding of French grew until eventually he could converse easily with the men and women he met in the settlement, even those who came to talk politics with Dumont in an excited staccato. He listened to this talk with increasing discomfort and knew Tante Madeleine agreed with him. For although she said nothing, she inevitably banged her pots as she worked in the kitchen, especially when she heard the name Louis Riel.

Ben first met Riel not long after he and Red Eagle returned from Fort Carlton with Charity's books. The Métis leader rode up to the cabin alone one morning while they dug potatoes and piled them in baskets. Without being told, Ben knew who the rider was, for he had heard much about the fiery Riel. Dumont was the respected leader, but Riel was almost revered in the settlements along both branches of the Saskatchewan River. He was of medium height and build with thick, wavy dark hair and the usual moustache and beard to match, though, unlike Dumont, Riel kept his well trimmed. Although seven years younger than Dumont, who bemoaned the fact he was nearing fifty, Riel appeared older due to the perpetually sad expression in his dark brown eyes.

It was after Riel's third appearance at the cabin that Tante Madeleine openly questioned the judgement of her husband in siding with this man. Dumont hadn't attended the big assembly of the Métis council in St. Laurent the day before, and Riel's eyes glowed as he strode up and down, gesturing wildly. "I tell you, my friend, we are together in this—whites, Métis, and Indians. And you and I will lead them to a new nation separate from Canada."

Dumont frowned. "This is the first I have heard of a new nation."

Riel stopped pacing and reached out to grab his friend's shoulders. "Nothing is impossible. Our friend William Jackson will apply directly to England for recognition for us. We owe no allegiance to Canada, for did it not break its promise to give us provincial status? Does it not instead take our land, control our resources, and ignore our delegates to Ottawa? Think of it, Gabriel, we can create a great country of our own with Métis traditions and Métis government!"

"For certain, Louis," Dumont began slowly, "it is a fine dream, but think now. Jackson of Prince Albert speaks for the whites, and maybe a little for the Métis, but I have heard this man, and the Indians mean nothing to him. Would you abandon the people of our grandmothers?"

"Gabriel! Is there something wrong with your hearing? I tell you, we are in this together—all who live along the rivers as well as our Indian brothers. Even now Jackson rides to the houses and farms of the English settlements and then will go to the French parishes to get signed authorizations for him to be the delegate to speak for us in England. Before we are finished Ottawa will pay us for the land they took from us. And then they will leave us in peace."

Dumont stroked his beard as he eyed the other man. "You find money very important, do you not, Louis?"

"Yes, of course."

"Is it true you agreed to leave us for Quebec or Montana if you were paid a good sum by those in Ottawa?"

The light died in Riel's eyes, and his usual sad expression returned as he glanced at the corner where Tante Madeleine knitted quietly. "I see Father André has been here gossiping."

"It is true then?"

Riel stood and began to pace again, this time slowly. "It is true, and it is not. For our great cause it is necessary to use trickery and lies as our enemies do. I would have agreed to leave for a few thousand dollars, money that would mean little to the government of Canada. I would have used the money to start a newspaper in North Dakota. With it, nothing would stop us from getting word to all our people when we rise to do battle. And with words for weapons we could stir the Americans to aid us in our cause." He spun on his heel and bent over Dumont. "Gabriel, old friend, if you doubt me, I will go now and never return."

Dumont took a deep breath. "No, you would not lie to me, and you must not leave. You are needed here. I will explain this to Father André."

"No," Riel said quickly. "Not yet. Face it, Gabriel, it is possible that old man may not be trusted completely." He pulled on his lip and muttered, "The time may come when what Father André does is unimportant, for much is to be looked at here, including what we have been led to believe is the one church."

Tante Madeleine gasped and her face grew pale, but she said nothing until the door closed behind Riel. Her skirts whirled around her as she turned, and her eyes blazed as she looked up at her husband. "Did you hear that, Gabriel? I warned you he would go too far. Now he mocks a priest who has cared for our people these many years as though we were his children, and he challenges our belief in our church!"

Ben felt Charity's hand tremble on his arm. When Tante Madeleine sometimes scolded her husband for neglecting to take off his muddy boots or for putting his feet on the table, he would sweep her off her feet and run around the room in circles until she laughed and forgot why she was angry. This time Dumont stood still and stared back at her in stiff-necked silence.

To Ben's relief, there was a firm knock on the door. He yanked it open, and Poundmaker raised a hand in greeting.

FIVE

As he stepped inside, the chief dropped the shabby red Hudson's Bay blanket from his shoulders. Fleetingly Ben thought any other Indian might look ridiculous in a white man's coat with frayed sleeves that were too short and britches to match. But Poundmaker's dignity filled the room. Tante Madeleine took Charity's hand, and together they went into the kitchen to prepare food for their distinguished visitor while Dumont, with a gesture, ushered the chief to a buffalo robe on the floor. Together they sat cross-legged in front of the fire. Beckoning to Ben, Red Eagle chose a spot close to the wall beside the open fireplace where he could watch Poundmaker's face and tell Ben what was said.

The chief had touched Red Eagle's shoulders briefly in passing and had smiled warmly at Ben before he seated himself and began to speak. "Riel has sent a messenger to the camps of our people to tell us the time may come when we must fight for our right to live," Red Eagle translated. "I tell you, my friend Gabriel, I do not wish to offend this Riel, but my eyes have looked upon the terrible plight of Sitting Bull and his warriors who defeated Custer almost ten years ago. If we, too, defeat one general or ten generals, it is possible we may have to move from place to place, begging for food and a piece of land to raise our tents as the Sioux do now. It is difficult to believe there is that which is worse than the hunger and cold my people suffer, but my heart tells me it is true."

The round clock on the wall ticked off the minutes as the two men stared into the fire. Finally Dumont spoke. "The time may come when we must fight, but I have counselled Riel to wait until all else fails. A few telegraph lines cut here and there, a piece of track removed to keep trains from the West, horses spirited away in the night from the forts—these things would make it difficult for this prime minister with the neck of a goose to complete his plans for settling the West and cause him to listen to our requests. Even John Macdonald must agree we should have rights just as his friends in the East do. It is possible he does not understand we do not have these rights yet. We will do what we must to make him listen."

Poundmaker continued to gaze into the fire. "Even now as we speak, in my camp there are old ones who cough until blood comes, and little ones who cry from cold and hunger. I cannot wait."

"What will you do, my friend?" Dumont asked.

"I rode to Battleford to talk with the Indian agent, but he is not there. I have learned that Superintendent Crozier is at Fort Carlton. He is a fair man and knows I speak only what is true. He may be able to persuade the Indian agent to give us blankets and more food for the winter." He paused for a moment, then added, "I have come here first to ask if you will ride with me to the fort."

"It is late," Dumont said, getting to his feet. "Come, we will have food and talk more in front of the fire. In the morning we will start early."

Riel was going faster than Dumont felt necessary, Ben thought. This might be the kind of information his uncle should hear. It might help prevent trouble for Dumont and Tante Madeleine and the rest of the settlements. Before he lost his courage, Ben blurted, "Gabriel, could I ride over to the fort with you? I'd like to ask if there's news of my father."

Tante Madeleine emerged from the kitchen with a platter of roasted venison. She placed it on the table and, with hands on hips, glared at her husband. "And do I understand you plan another journey?"

"Do not fret, my treasure," Dumont said. "I will not be absent so long this time. It is less than three hours on the trail to Fort Carlton. We will talk a little, then I will return as straight as a bee to his hive." He winked at Ben. "It is time we pay a call on your uncle. It may be wise to learn if the strength of the Mounted Police is as much as he has said to you."

Ben nodded and tried to think of something else. Anything else.

In the morning Charity announced she wished to gather the eggs herself and asked Ben if he would help before he left. He agreed, fully aware that Charity's purpose was to get him alone. In the barn she said, "Ben, I hate to see you go to the fort with Gabriel. I meant to tell you I learned Uncle Lawrence detests him because of some trouble they had a long time ago."

"How'd you hear that?"

"I'm blind, not deaf," Charity retorted. "Tante Madeleine and her friends talk about a lot of things while their husbands are at their endless meetings." She giggled. "One day I heard Tante Madeleine say if Lawrence Clarke thought it might help Hudson's Bay save money, he'd go naked in the winter and expect the clerks to do the same."

Ben's hoot of laughter sent chickens squawking for cover. When he stopped, he said, "I expect she's right, but that doesn't change the fact that trouble for the company could hurt the Métis, too. What happened? Do you know?"

"I asked Father André about it while he waited here for Tante Madeleine to return from Mr. Letendre's store in Batoche. He said it happened about ten years ago when there was no government at all here. He said the people felt they should have some rules to live by, so they made the St. Laurent Council with Gabriel Dumont as president."

"I heard he was elected president," Ben said. "And the laws they made were about the same as the ones for the big buffalo hunts they used to have."

Charity's head bobbed up and down. "I expect so. Anyway, Father André said there weren't many violations because the Métis respect each other's rights. But one of the most important laws was that nobody could go on a buffalo hunt before they all got together to go at the same time. And that's just what three Métis men did. They went hunting with two other men who weren't Métis, and when the council heard about it, they went after them. They took away the guns and supplies of the three Métis because they had signed the council agreement and knew that was the punishment, but they left the other men alone."

"But what's that got to do with Uncle Lawrence? He wasn't one of the other men, was he?"

Charity giggled again. "Oh, Ben, can you see Uncle Lawrence shooting from a horse thundering through a herd of stampeding buffalo?"

"And how'd you get to know so much about stampeding buffalo?"

"Same as you. I listen to Gabriel's stories, too." Charity shook her head. "Now please listen, Ben. Father André said the Métis men accepted their punishment, but the other two went to Fort Carlton to see Uncle Lawrence. He'd just been appointed justice of the peace for miles around, and you know how he likes to feel important. So you can imagine how furious he was about the whole thing. He was the law, and he resented Gabriel for acting as though he and his council had the right to decide what's right and what's wrong. He sent for help, and fifty Mounted Police went after the Métis council."

"Was Gabriel arrested?"

"No, Gabriel and his officers apologized and gave back the guns and equipment. But they told the colonel in charge—I think his name was French—that because they had no other government, they'd made their own and thought they were being fair."

Ben scratched his head thoughtfully. "That's a puny thing for Uncle Lawrence to be mad about for ten years. After all, Gabriel apologized, didn't he? And it seems to me he tried to do the right thing."

"That's not all of it, Ben. The newspaper in Regina heard about Uncle Lawrence asking for fifty policemen and printed big headlines about a terrible Indian uprising out here with people killed and forts burned. It made the government look silly when they found that wasn't true. Father André said this Colonel French gave Uncle Lawrence a dressing-down in front of everyone in Fort Carlton. He told him everybody would be better off if he left the Métis to their own devices and just took care of Hudson's Bay."

Ben whistled under his breath. He could see how that would stick in his uncle's craw, all right. Even his mother had once said that Uncle Lawrence's pride could be tiresome.

They made good time riding to Fort Carlton, for the river was frozen enough to ride across and wagons on the trail had packed the snow, making it easy for their horses to move at a fast walk. Without Red Eagle there was no one to translate the bits of conversation between his companions until Dumont turned to Ben to explain. "Poundmaker wishes to learn more of my grandfather, who was the first of the Dumonts to ride this prairie."

There was a note of pride in Dumont's voice as he continued. "I told him my grandfather, Jean-Baptiste Dumont, paddled from Montreal in his *bateau* and wed a tall, strong Sarcee woman who gave him three big sons. One was my father, Isidore. With him and his brother, Jean, I went to Devil's Lake one time when they tried to make peace with the leaders of the Sioux. I was only a boy, and a Sioux hit me on my head with his gun. For this he was punished by his chief. At camp my Uncle Jean gave me my first rifle—one with a short barrel. I called it Le Petit." Dumont stared straight ahead, riding silently for a time before he spoke again. "Four years later, before a buffalo hunt, I used Le Petit against the Sioux in the Battle of Grand Coteau. I have had bigger guns since, but all are Le Petit."

In response to a question from Ben, Dumont said, "I was born beside the river at St. Boniface. My blessed mother died of consumption in the same year your Tante Madeleine and I were wed by a priest in North Dakota. My father married again—a woman from Red River. He lives north of Batoche and would be here to help us, but he has been very sick."

There were more stories of his youth, and when Dumont turned his attention to Poundmaker, Ben mulled over what he had heard. It was easy to see why the Métis people had elected Dumont their leader. He had been successful as a trapper and a freighter. And before he sold it, his ferryboat was a real money-maker. People still talked of his fame as a buffalo hunter. There was a glow of pride in Ben's heart that he now rode beside such a man.

A little later, when his uncle greeted Dumont and Poundmaker inside the fort without incident, Ben sighed with relief. In fact, Uncle Lawrence appeared to be in good spirits. When Dumont politely refused his offer to dine at the house, opting instead to accompany Poundmaker in his search for Superintendent Crozier, the chief factor grabbed Ben's arm and tugged him up the steps to his office. "Well," he demanded when they were safely inside, "what have you learned? Why is Dumont here?"

"Poundmaker asked him to come with him to see Superintendent Crozier."

Clarke's pale eyes stared at Ben. "Well, have you nothing to tell me? What's Riel up to?"

Although Ben was prepared for the question, he wondered now if his uncle would be satisfied with his response. He cleared his throat. "Gabriel Dumont doesn't hold with some of Riel's ideas about how to push the government into agreeing with what they want. He thinks they're getting somewhere now that the people in Winnipeg sent their petition on to Ottawa." Ignoring his uncle's grimace, he added, "I think the Métis are mostly afraid they'll end up cheated out of their land again the way they were in Manitoba."

Clarke waved his hand in front of the sardonic smile on his face. "Yes, yes, I've heard all that many times—the poor, poor Métis. If the truth be known, most of them likely gambled away their land."

Ben resisted the temptation to argue. Instead, he rose and said, "I best see if Gabriel's ready to leave." Then, remembering his manners, he asked, "And how's your family?"

The apologetic response Ben got surprised him. "They're well. Your aunt said to give you her best whenever I see you and wants you to know we'd have sent for you and your sister to have Christmas with us, but we feared with the cold trip Charity might have sickened again. I know you both must have felt homesick for your own kind, but I trust the day was agreeable."

Ben nodded. Christmas Day had been spent quietly after church, but on New Year's Eve and for a week after they had feasted at one Métis house after another, singing loudly as the carriage crunched over the snow. The holiday celebration was in sharp contrast to the one he would have enjoyed far less in St. Albert with his prim and proper aunt and his cousins.

Thinking about how little his uncle really cared about

their welfare, Ben looked at the man with a sudden surge of resentment. "Charity was truly happy with a book about Christmas that one of the priests gave her. He got it from a policeman in charge of Fort Pitt. It was written by an Englishman named Dickens."

"Oh, indeed, very kind, very kind," the chief factor said, a note of dismissal in his voice as he began to stack some papers on the desk.

Ben stood abruptly, feeling suffocated in the tiny office. "I have to find Gabriel."

Clarke's chair scraped the floor and tipped backward when he, too, got to his feet hastily. His tone was a shade too hearty as he held out his hand. "Goodbye then, Ben. You've done well. I'll send another telegram urging the government to heed the requests of the St. Laurent Council, and at the same time advise them to send additional troops to all the forts along both branches of the river."

Ben was certain the information he had given his uncle made little difference. A telegram from Lawrence Clarke advising the government to do anything would probably be ignored. Nevertheless, he left with a heavy heart, for now he had to face the best man he had ever known and pretend his only reason to see his uncle was to learn if there had been news of his father. Even if it was to keep Charity safe at Gabriel's Crossing, he would rather die than have Dumont know he was a liar.

Suddenly realizing there was a small possibility that his uncle's request for troops might be granted, Ben stumbled heedlessly down the steps and through the door, scarcely feeling the numbing cold that iced the sweat on his face. More well-armed North-West Mounted Police on the posts might not stop the Métis now that their hopes were so high. If there were a fight, they could be outnumbered, and for sure they wouldn't have the weapons they needed. They could face disaster.

SIX

The temperature plunged and the wind shrieked down the river valley, driving the snow before it into glistening mounds against fences and outbuildings to create a stark white landscape bare of life. Ben was thankful he had brought his father's treasured spyglass, for without it to scan the horizons for smoke from the chimneys of his neighbours, Dumont would have ridden in the numbing cold to make certain they were still alive.

The storms had begun two days after Poundmaker parted from them at Fort Carlton, and time and time again, Ben wondered if the chief had made it to his lodge before the first blizzard began. Poundmaker had seemed cheerful after his talk with Superintendent Crozier, and on the ride back to the Crossing, Dumont had told Ben that the superintendent had promised to telegraph his superiors in Regina to see if they could urge the Department of Indian Affairs to send extra food. Also, the wives of the Mounted Police officers were writing to friends back east, urging them to form an organization to gather blankets and clothing to be distributed in the reserves. Crozier had cautioned, however, that times were very bad for all of Canada right now, so they must not expect too much.

When February arrived, the almost daily storms grew weaker and gradually died. At that time men from the St. Laurent Council began to arrive at the Dumonts' cabin in twos and threes to discuss their growing anger. It was taking much too long for a response from the government to their final petition. During one of these discussions, Riel burst into the room excitedly. "Soon we shall have an answer to our cry for justice. Father André sent off a letter to Ottawa demanding they reply to our petition. I have seen it for myself. At last he, too, has run out of patience. I believe it is possible now to allow him to hold his position in our new order."

Standing beside Red Eagle in the kitchen doorway, Ben darted a glance behind him at Tante Madeleine, who stared tight-lipped out a window of her kitchen. She turned her head and, as her eyes met his, she murmured, "I wish to thank you for coming here with Charity, for these past months have been happy ones and may be the last Gabriel and I will have."

Charity rose from her stool beside the stove and reached out aimlessly with both hands. "Oh, Tante Madeleine, you mustn't believe that! You know what Gabriel said last night. The people talk angrily, but they're farmers now, not warriors. They'll be patient."

A wry smile lifted one corner of Tante Madeleine's mouth, but her voice was soft when she took Charity's hands. "Of course, *chérie*, you are right. It is, but when I hear talk of this new order and of removing our priests, I am concerned. For me, such words are blasphemy. Perhaps, though, nothing will happen."

Tante Madeleine was proven to be wrong when near the end of February a young messenger arrived with word of an important meeting at St. Antoine Church in Batoche. Every man had to be there.

As Dumont bid his wife goodbye, he grinned and cautioned her and Charity to behave themselves while the menfolk piously went to church. Later, his expression became increasingly grim as he and the two boys pushed their horses to a fast walk during the hourlong ride to the little church just north of Batoche. Although the church was already crowded when they arrived, Ben and Red Eagle managed to shoulder their way to a place along the wall. Men moved to make a pathway for Dumont to stride to the front and seat himself on a bench beside Riel and the other leaders of the St. Laurent Council. Father Moulin and Father Vegreville stood on the low altar behind the men. For so many people in one room, it was strangely quiet. Ben scanned the faces and noted that most of them wore anxious expressions, but a few had their jaws set in determination. His attention turned to the front of the church as Riel rose.

"We have our answer," the Métis said, surveying the faces in front of him. "Generously Canada has agreed to send three men to investigate the claims of those who did not get a land grant."

Laughter rose from the audience, and someone said jeeringly, "They are generous with talk and nothing else."

Riel didn't smile. After a dramatic pause, he continued. "Not only will we not have provincial status for this land, but they have ignored our request for Métis representation in either the Territorial Council or the Canadian Senate." A wave of angry whispers swept through the audience, and Riel held up a hand for silence. "Also, the request that our land be resurveyed was not granted. In short, my friends, not one petition for ourselves or our Indian brothers has been considered."

For a long moment the listening men sat stunned. Then, as one, they rose, waving their fists and shouting insults at Macdonald and Dewdney. The priests left the altar and, without raising their voices, circulated among the men until order was restored and the shouts were reduced to sullen mutters. Riel, head bowed, began to speak again. "I have failed you. It is time for me to return to Montana, for all my efforts have come to nothing."

"No! No! No!" filled the room until Riel raised his head. Ben felt a shiver along his spine when he saw the light burning in the Métis's eyes.

"You are my people," Riel began softly, "and I will be your leader in this battle." His words grew louder as he repeatedly reminded them to expect more drastic actions, finishing with, "If we are forced to, we will declare this land a new nation under God as I once did in Manitoba."

The crowd roared its approval, but a frowning Father Vegreville strode back to the altar and raised his hands. "What you counsel is treason, Louis Riel. Those who followed you in Manitoba escaped punishment only because at that time you had no government there. Here we have a territorial government. And if the Métis defy it, they could face death by hanging. Is this what you want?"

Riel was silent for a moment, then said, "What I will bring to my people is the right to live secure in the knowledge that the cabins they build and the land they clear are theirs to keep and then pass on to their children and their grandchildren after them. Is it so much to ask that a man be free to work his land without fearing all will be taken from him?"

Ben was impressed by the sincerity in Riel's voice, but the priest shook his head vigorously. "Louis, there are many ways a man can lose everything he has worked hard for. Be careful what you do."

Riel appeared to agree that day, but two weeks later the thunder of hoof beats announced his arrival at Dumont's cabin with sixty armed men. Ben and Red Eagle ran down from the barn and halted halfway as Dumont opened the cabin door. Riel cried, "I have learned the police want me, but we no longer recognize the authority of the police here." He swept one arm in the direction of the other riders. "These men are with me to the end!"

Conflicting emotions flickered in Dumont's eyes, but he said nothing. Riel waved the hand-size wooden cross he carried and said, "Come, my general, we ride to Halcro for a meeting with the English-speaking Métis. It is time for action."

As Ben listened, his stomach churned, then he glanced sideways to see Red Eagle look at him with curiosity. "You are afraid?" the Cree asked.

Ben nodded. "Look around, Red Eagle. Gabriel's got horses and cattle and money from freighting and selling the ferry. He and Tante Madeleine are doing just fine, but they could lose it all if Gabriel bucks the Mounted Police."

"The police are few, the Métis and Indians are many more."

"They'll bring more. Maybe even the army. What'll we do then?"

"We will do what we must."

The full import of Red Eagle's words struck Ben hard, and he faced his friend with wide, frightened eyes. Red Eagle would fight beside his people; he might even be killed. And what about Tante Madeleine, and Charity, too, if there was a war? Much as he disliked Uncle Lawrence, he hoped the man might be right: if the Métis realized they faced overwhelming numbers of well-armed police, perhaps, for the sake of their families, they would have enough sense to back down.

Dumont responded to Riel in a tone too low for Ben to hear, but as the big man stepped back, he said clearly, "Ride ahead. I will join you tonight at Halcro."

With shouts of farewell the men left, spattering clumps of slush from the hooves of their horses. Ben entered the cabin behind Dumont to see Tante Madeleine packing the saddle-bags her husband took on his trips away from home. Her lips were pressed tightly, and she didn't look up at them.

Dumont clasped her shoulders and turned her around. "Tell me what you would have me do. I am an old lion now with worn teeth and claws no longer sharp, but still the people look to me to lead." When his wife didn't answer, he said, "I will not go without your blessing."

Ben's chest filled with pain when he saw tears gather in the corners of Tante Madeleine's eyes. She looked up at her husband. "Where will you lead our neighbours and friends? To destruction?"

Dumont shook his shaggy head. "No, this I swear to you. I will counsel them not to be hasty, but to be cautious."

"And if Riel does not listen?"

"Then I will agree only to lead men on raids here and there where no one will be hurt—perhaps not even the enemy."

Tante Madeleine's smile failed to reach her eyes. "Go then with my blessing."

Almost a week passed before Dumont returned. His usually ready grin appeared forced as he greeted them in the cabin, and he had little to say. From the kitchen Tante Madeleine brought in a plate heaped with potatoes and crisp slices of baked pork. When Dumont began to eat, she said, "A novena begins tomorrow. We will pray for a way out of our trouble."

"We need the prayers," Dumont said.

Ben couldn't stand the waiting any longer. "Gabriel, what happened at the meeting? Will the men wait before they fight?"

Dumont shook his head, and his tone was bitter. "I warned Riel and the council that the whites and many of our English-speaking people are not yet ready for talk of war. They have retreated to their houses like frightened rabbits and tell us they do not want an Indian war. Except for our Indian brothers, we may be alone."

"What about Mr. Jackson?" Ben asked. "Did he go to England to see the queen?"

Dumont scowled. "I am told Jackson has been very sick."

"But what will we do?" Tante Madeleine cried. "We are too

few to create a storm big enough for the government to take notice."

Beside Ben, Red Eagle said, "We will be enough."

Dumont shrugged. "I have tried to counsel our people wisely. Perhaps I have failed."

"Who was at the meeting?" Ben prodded anxiously. "What was decided?"

"We met with Riel, Joseph Ouelette and his son, Moise, the brothers Pierre and Philippe Gariepey, John Ross, Augustin Laframboise, Calixte Lafontaine, Napoleon Nault..."

As Dumont reeled off the names, Ben tried to give them faces, for most of the men had likely come to the cabin at one time or another. But all he could be sure of was that they were members of the Métis Council.

"And two Dumonts—Isidore and me," the big man finished. "We signed the oath. We will fight."

Ben felt Charity clutch his arm and heard Tante Madeleine's swift intake of breath as Dumont continued. "Even though Riel says we fight for the glory of God, some believe we should have a few days of prayer. I feel this, as well. After that, each man will be free to walk in the path he is certain God wishes him to take."

In the morning Red Eagle went to the barn to saddle a horse while Dumont hurriedly ate his porridge. When he finished, he rose and touched Ben's shoulder. "I will be in Batoche for not more than two days. If I am needed, send Red Eagle."

Wordlessly Dumont bent to kiss Charity's forehead, then reached out a hand to his wife. Wrapped in her heavy black shawl, Tante Madeleine followed her husband outside to watch until he rode out of sight.

Ben seized this moment alone with his sister. "If ever Ottawa's going to send reinforcements, it better be now. I best ride to the fort."

Charity's face twisted. "Oh, Ben, are you sure?"

"I'm not sure of anything anymore, except it looks like

Riel's made up his mind. He's the one persuading the council they have to fight. I've thought about this a lot, Charity. It's a gamble. If Uncle Lawrence sends word to Winnipeg that the Métis are ready to fight, the government just might hurry up and give them some of the rights they've asked for."

"And if they don't?"

Ben's lips tightened. "If they believe Uncle this time, I guess they'll send troops. Lots of troops. If that happens, I hope Riel will hightail it back to Montana and this will quiet down." He swallowed hard. "I can't just sit here and wish, Charity. I have to do something."

"I…I expect you're right. But, Ben, what if Uncle Lawrence isn't there?"

"Then I'll leave a message with McKay, the chief trader."

Getting away from the cabin for a day without giving an elaborate excuse was no problem, for Dumont was absent again and Tante Madeleine had become increasingly withdrawn. The tension eased in her face only when she paused to speak to Charity. Red Eagle, however, was another problem. Sick of deception, Ben said bluntly, "I've got to ride to Fort Carlton, Red Eagle, so I'm hoping you don't mind doing the chores alone. If I'm not back before sundown, it means I'm staying the night."

Red Eagle's trusting expression only served to increase Ben's guilt, but he shook it off as his horse cantered across the snow-covered prairie. The river ice had thinned dangerously, but downstream there was a low spot the settlers commonly used in the spring before the melting snow and ice from the mountains surged eastward and raised the rushing water to a flood. Frost formed on the edges of his nostrils, and his fingers stiffened with cold, but Ben barely noticed. Instead, he concentrated on what he had to say when he arrived at the fort.

Uncle Lawrence had returned to the fort only hours before, and he greeted Ben warmly. As he rushed his nephew into the office, he said, "I'm eager to hear what you have to tell me. I understand the Métis are more defiant than ever and are even refusing to haul freight for our company or work for the government."

"An oath's been signed to fight," Ben began, the words tumbling from his mouth. "But Louis Riel scared off the whites and some of the English-speaking Métis by stirring up the Indians. The whites don't want the Indian people to be part of anything."

Clarke strode up and down the small room, his eyes bright with triumph. "I knew it! I warned Dewdney, but he wouldn't listen! I had to take it upon myself to get more protection for the fort, and have sent McKay to Prince Albert for volunteers." He whirled and probed Ben's eyes with his own. "What else? Are the rest of the Métis behind Riel? How many men does he have?"

"I don't know. Some of the Métis families have gone away until the trouble is over, and some left because of what Riel says about the church."

Clarke nodded. "I heard." His lip curled in a sneer. "Riel's trying to convince them the Lord will come to their aid because he was ordained to be the prophet of the new world. Blasphemy! The man should be whipped!"

"I don't know about that." Even though Riel made Ben feel uncomfortable, he didn't doubt the man believed in his mission. And how was someone supposed to know if a fellow was a prophet or not? Noticing the expectant look on Clarke's face, Ben continued hastily before his uncle could question his feelings for the Métis. "I mean, the priests turned against Riel. They don't want him to use the church to make speeches, and that's what made him think about a new church, I guess."

"What's Dumont doing now?"

Ben shifted in his chair uneasily. It was one thing to tell his uncle about the situation in general, but quite another to inform on Gabriel Dumont specifically, so he hedged. "I don't know where he is this minute—home maybe."

"I took the ferry at Batoche this morning and found men meeting in Letendre's store, but there was no sign of Dumont," Clarke said. The gleam was back in his eyes, and there was a ring of victory in his voice. "Go back and tell that arrogant buffalo hunter that I've returned from Winnipeg where I learned that Colonel Irvine, with a force of Mounted Police larger than he can imagine, is on his way to arrest him and Riel and the rest of their followers. They'll soon learn the price of treason."

Ben was startled. "That's true? They'll arrest Gabriel?"

If Clarke had noticed his nephew's concern for Dumont, he gave no sign. "Ride back and tell the Métis what I've told you. There's still time for them to return to their jobs and forget this treasonable nonsense."

SEVEN

Tante Madeleine came to greet Ben at the door when he returned from Fort Carlton. Over her head he saw Dumont seated near the blazing fire. The man appeared haggard and drawn, but his smile was as broad as ever and his voice boomed a welcome.

Knowing he couldn't bring himself to lie to Dumont, Ben gambled no one would question his reasons for riding to the fort because they would be more concerned about the warning he brought. He was right. When he reported that an army of Mounted Police was on its way to arrest the council members, Tante Madeleine cried out and Dumont leaped to his feet to reach for Le Petit in the corner. Over his shoulder he called to Red Eagle, "Saddle a fresh horse. I ride to Batoche."

The Cree boy disappeared through the door in a flash, and Tante Madeleine flew to the kitchen to prepare a packet of food.

"Ben," Charity said, grabbing his arm, "what will happen? Gabriel won't be arrested, will he?"

"No, of course not. Uncle Lawrence said if everyone settles down, the police will likely go back soon enough. Gabriel just wants to warn Riel and the rest."

That night Ben tossed and turned on his pallet as he tried to fall asleep. When the door creaked open, he sat up and peered over the edge of the loft to see Dumont slip off his boots and pad across the room to the curtained alcove below. Ben turned on his side and burrowed under his blankets. He felt better. Maybe Dumont and the council had made plans to go away until things settled down. Maybe bringing back his information from the fort had saved Tante Madeleine and Dumont from something terrible.

Before daybreak Ben woke with a start when he heard both Dumonts moving about the cabin quietly in the dark. In the kitchen they lit a small lantern. Ben scrambled into his clothes, and nearby Red Eagle stirred.

"*Bien*," Dumont said when the two boys appeared. "We have work to do today. Bring your rifles and blankets, for we will be away more than a day."

"We will hunt?" Red Eagle asked.

Dumont smiled, but his eyes were cold. "We will hunt, but for weapons, not meat. Riel is right. The time has come to defend ourselves."

Uncle Lawrence was wrong. The Métis were going to fight. They were going to fight an army of policemen. Ben's lips felt like ice, and his throat was too dry to speak. He stumbled behind Red Eagle to roll up his bedroll and take his rifle from the pegs in the wall above the fireplace. He was vaguely aware that Charity was moving around behind the curtains of her alcove.

"Ben!" she called as she pushed aside the curtain and appeared wearing a heavy blue corduroy robe over her night-clothes. "Is everyone up? It seems early."

Red Eagle moved to her instantly, took her hand, and led her to the table. Tante Madeleine had already brought in a large brown teapot with steam curling upward from its spout, then returned to the kitchen to stir the pot of porridge she had cooked the night before and reheated for the morning meal. Her face was serene and her shoulders squared as she moved back and forth, seemingly resigned to whatever might happen.

"It's early all right," Ben muttered, sitting on the bench beside his twin. He waited until Tante Madeleine was in a muffled conversation with Dumont before he whispered, "It didn't work, Charity. Uncle Lawrence was all wrong. The Métis plan to fight even if a thousand Mounted Police come."

"Fight? Oh, Ben, you, too, and Red Eagle?"

"I...I don't think so. Not just yet, but Gabriel said we need more guns and ammunition so we can defend ourselves if the police come after us."

The distress on Charity's face disappeared. "All the talk here is about defending the land, not about attacking the police. And you know as well as I do that Superintendent Crozier and his men won't come here to shoot at these people. It'll be the way Uncle Lawrence said—a way to make everyone stop and think and talk until everything's settled."

Ben took a deep breath, then released it. "I hope you're right, Charity, but I already decided from here on I'm going to leave it to Gabriel to figure out what's best. And if I see Uncle Lawrence again, I'm going to tell him so. As far as I'm concerned, he can just put that in his pipe and smoke it!"

After breakfast, Ben, Red Eagle, and Dumont went to the barn. Once inside, the big Métis looked at Ben and said, "Hitch the two bays to the wagon and tie your horse behind."

The three of them worked quickly, warming the bridle bits in their hands before forcing them into reluctant muzzles. In minutes Red Eagle and Dumont were trotting down the trail to Batoche along the bluffs above the river, with Ben following in the wagon.

His heart thumping, Ben muttered the same plea repeatedly under his breath. “Talk, not fight. Talk, not fight.” Then he heard an unidentifiable rumble in the still air. As the noise grew, he made out the clatter of shod hoofs striking frozen ground. A moment later a band of more than sixty horsemen, led by Louis Riel, burst over the horizon.

Ben pulled his team to a halt, and Red Eagle backed up his horse until it stood beside the wagon. “What are they doing?” Ben asked, watching the riders bunch together as they listened in silence to Dumont.

Red Eagle shook his head. “I cannot hear.”

Dumont spoke briefly, then signalled Ben. “Come.”

Their destination was a long, peeled log cabin that served as a residence and store. Dumont halted the men a hundred yards away and chose three to accompany him as he went on to the store. The rest of the riders stared after them while Ben stood on the wagon seat to watch. Dumont and his three companions dropped the reins over the heads of their horses and went inside. Minutes later they emerged, guns in hand pointed at two men who walked ahead of them.

“Who are they?” Ben asked Red Eagle.

Riel’s ears were good, for he turned and called over his shoulder, “The Indian agent for One Arrow Reserve and his interpreter.” He gathered his reins and added, “Bring the wagon, my young friend. We are here for weapons.”

Dumont detailed ten men to haul the arms and ammunition out of the store, then ordered Red Eagle to bring the horses belonging to the two prisoners. Red Eagle seemed puzzled as he dismounted. “That one is a good Indian agent. He is like Jefferson on our reserve. He helps as much as he can.”

Dumont clapped him on the shoulder. “They will come to no harm. But since they work for the government, we may be able to use them to bargain.”

“What about the storekeeper?” Ben asked uneasily. The man hadn’t appeared.

"Monsieur Storekeeper is quite safe inside, but it is understandable he is a little sad." Dumont gestured at the pile of weapons in the wagon. "We promised to return everything if it is not needed."

Although this was the same smiling Dumont he knew well, Ben sensed a new, heightened confidence and authority. Perhaps Dumont hadn't felt useful in all the petition writing and meetings, but now the people had turned to him to lead in a fight, something he did well.

The two prisoners didn't seem that upset with their situation. They chatted with their captors freely as they rode on to Batoche and a second store, which wasn't owned by Métis. There they liberated a large supply of weapons and ammunition. However, the owner objected so strenuously that Dumont decided to take him as a hostage, although some of the men doubted the government would bargain to get back a man who used such bad language.

"Take the prisoners to Batoche," Dumont commanded the two men who guarded them. "And see that they get food and water. When I return, we will decide where they will be kept." He beckoned to Ben, and with the rest of the band walking their horses behind the wagon, followed the double track in the snow to the green two-story house of Xavier Letendre. When Riel and most of the men dismounted in front, Dumont turned aside and followed a short trail to a row of three rough, unpainted sheds. There, he and Red Eagle leaped from their horses and opened the heavy double doors of the middle shed so Ben could drive the wagon inside.

"Now what?" Ben asked Dumont.

"Now, as your good uncle often says, we get down to business. Please take care of the horses and then join us inside the house Letendre so kindly left empty for us to use as our headquarters."

While they unhitched the team, Ben explained the situation to Red Eagle. "Old Letendre—Batoche, I guess some call him—

goes to Fort à la Corne to trade every winter, and Gabriel thinks this time he'll stay there until the trouble's over."

Leaving their own horses saddled, Ben and Red Eagle led them down to the hitching rail in front of the house. Then, together, they leaped up the front steps and entered a long, low-ceilinged room in time to see Riel raise his cross high over his head and proclaim, "Here we establish the Provisional Government of Saskatchewan!"

As the men cheered loudly, Red Eagle turned to Ben, his eyes glowing with excitement. "What does it mean?"

Ben groaned inwardly. "I hate to think what it means. First, they only want to defend their land, and now they're talking about taking the whole territory. This isn't good at all."

Red Eagle raised his chin proudly. "You are wrong, Ben. We will take back what Canada took from us. It is time."

The men were quiet again, and Riel said, "I nominate Gabriel Dumont to be adjutant general of the Métis nation and head of the army." After the roar of approval died, he put his hand on the shoulder of the oldest Métis in the room and added, "We have twelve men on our council and for president I now choose our wise friend, Pierre Parteneau." There was a chorus of dissent, and Riel held up his hand for quiet. "I will not shirk my duty to you, but I serve best as your spiritual leader and will guide you in all things as I prophesied."

Dumont moved forward to stand beside Riel. "There could be no better command than those who were leaders of our buffalo hunts in the old days." He gestured to two men seated at a long table. "You are captains of the scouts. Choose ten of the best riders and patrol both sides of the river." He looked around the room, his face grave. "This may be more dangerous than meeting the Sioux when we searched for buffalo, but this time we fight not for meat but for our families and all we hold dear in our hearts." Dumont nodded toward the window. "More men arrive as we speak. We must provide tents for those who will stay the night. Tomorrow we plan our attack."

Ben and Red Eagle slipped outside and watched the rest of the men file through the door. It occurred to Ben that no fear or worry showed on the faces passing by, only grim determination. No matter how many men Ottawa sent, they would fight. Even as his heart sank at the thought, he felt a wave of admiration for their courage.

Red Eagle started to speak, but halted abruptly as the door burst open and Dumont stalked out. Behind him Riel pleaded, "My general, it is not true I intend to take charge of the fighting. I ask only that we wait here in Batoche until they come to arrest us and thus reveal to the world how Canada treats our people."

Dumont paused, then turned around. "Louis, you ask me to be your general and I agree. But to be a general I must have three things. One, I must have men to fight. Two, I must have guns for the men to shoot. Three, I must have ammunition to put in the guns. We barely have weapons for two days of battle. Fort Carlton would be easy to take, for it was made to keep out those who steal, not men who know how to fight. Superintendent Crozier only has a few men there, but they have plenty of weapons that would be useful here, and I would prefer to take them before he gets reinforcements."

Riel studied his general for a moment, then said, "Perhaps we can compromise. We will try to take the fort without bloodshed. I will send word that we will not harm them if they give up peacefully."

Dumont frowned. "I will be surprised if Crozier agrees to surrender the fort without a fight, but do as you wish." He pointed in the direction of the ferry, where a knot of men stood talking. "There is Hillyard Mitchell. He is a trader at Duck Lake, and though he is not one of us, I think he is sympathetic to our cause. Let us ask him to carry the message to Crozier." Dumont then looked at Ben. "And if Mitchell will do that it would be good for you to go with him, Ben." Dumont's smile erased some of the care from his face as he added, "It would be a fine thing for me to have someone who will take care that I learn everything said by the Mounted Police and Mitchell."

Ben nodded and half hoped the Duck Lake trader would refuse to go to the fort.

EIGHT

Hillyard Mitchell didn't refuse, though. If anything, Ben thought he seemed eager to help any way he could to keep the lid on the cauldron that threatened to boil over. The horses kept to a steady canter, and Mitchell talked as they rode. "I sent word to Crozier two days ago to warn him if they make a foolish move, the Indians would mass together to help their Métis friends. Can't blame 'em. On the reserves they got so little, they figure a poor chance is better than none at all."

The apprehension Ben felt stifled any desire for conversation, but he made himself reply civilly to the questions put to him. When he explained why Lawrence Clarke's nephew and niece were living with the Métis, Mitchell chuckled and said, "Clarke and Dumont are about as opposite in this trouble as they can get. I expect you'd best try to stay out of it."

Ben nodded, then a thought struck him and he felt himself

grow cold. Pulling his horse to a stop, he blurted, "Mr. Mitchell, I figure my uncle forgets about us except when he sees us, and with this trouble brewing, he might say we got to come back to the fort. No matter what happens, Charity's better off where she is. If real trouble comes, I can get her to Prince Albert."

Mitchell studied Ben for a moment, then said, "I see what you mean. Well, we're almost there, so you best come on ahead with me, but you know the fort. It shouldn't be any trouble to keep out of your uncle's sight, should it?"

Relieved, Ben grinned. "Thanks, Mr. Mitchell. I'll do that."

"Just keep your eyes sharp, though, so you can follow when I leave."

Ben tied his horse outside the fort gates, and no one appeared to notice when he slipped inside; the place was crowded with soldiers and well-armed men dressed in clothes more suitable for farming. Mitchell tied his horse to a post in front of the quarters for the Mounted Police and went inside. A moment later he came out and looked around before he shouted, "Superintendent Crozier, a word with you, if you please!"

"Good to see you again, Mitchell," a voice boomed, and the red-haired, solidly built officer of the North-West Mounted Police strode from the trade room, one hand outstretched. Crozier, though of average height, was a commanding figure in his immaculate red uniform and highly polished boots.

Listening from behind one of the parked wagons across the square, Ben heard Crozier ask, "What are those people up to over on the south branch? Clarke tells me they're in open rebellion and demands I arrest the leaders."

Ben slipped closer to hear Mitchell reply, "You'll get nothing but trouble for your pains if you listen to Clarke. Maybe it's him that should be put away. Why he's the one got 'em stirred up in the first place with all his talk about an army of police coming to arrest 'em!"

Crozier lowered his voice and glanced over his shoulder at the big house across the square. "Best we move away a bit, else the man might see us and come out to put in his tuppence worth of advice."

As the two men moved slowly toward the gate, Ben ambled along behind the wagons, trying to look as though he had a right to be there. The superintendent said, "I learned this morning that Dumont's men gathered up arms from some stores. You have a fair supply in yours if I remember rightly."

The storekeeper nodded. "A good stock, but that's not the reason I'm here." He stopped and turned to face the other man. "Riel sent me to tell you he doesn't want trouble and thinks you and your men should return to Prince Albert to keep blood from being shed."

"What's that!" Crozier bellowed, his roar so loud that Ben stood rooted to the spot as everyone around him turned to stare. The superintendent choked and sputtered and finally growled, "The fool must be daft! The North-West Mounted Police doesn't run from a ragtag mob of buffalo hunters or anyone else!"

Ben couldn't hear Mitchell's reply, but the man spoke for a long time, and the superintendent continued to scowl. Finally Crozier nodded, then beckoned to a young constable nearby. "Go fetch McKay," he ordered. To Mitchell he added, "He's just returned from Prince Albert with forty-three volunteers—the shopkeepers and clerks you see stumbling around here. Clarke's idea, of course. They'll likely be about as much help to us as lace trim on our rifles."

When the chief trader hurried up to the two men, Crozier said, "You understand these people. Best go back with Mitchell and see if you can reason with Riel. He wants us to hand over the fort to him." He jerked one thumb in the direction of a cannon chained in the bed of a wagon. "Tell him we have a seven-pounder with all the shot we need. Tell him if he shows up around here, I'll take pleasure in putting in the powder and adding the ball myself to blow him to kingdom come!"

Ben wasn't concerned about McKay joining them on the return to Batoche; the chief trader would most likely take it for granted that Ben had been to see his uncle. Whistling softly, Ben walked through the gates to his horse. When the two men rode out, he swung in beside them and nodded a greeting to McKay, who blinked once, then ignored him.

The Métis didn't trust McKay. To make matters worse, the chief trader, tired and out of sorts, grumbled that he had just ridden all the way from Prince Albert. Ben thought sending him to parley with Riel and Gabriel would be a waste of time.

The two Métis leaders, with McKay and Mitchell, were inside the store beside the Batoche ferry for less than an hour when McKay opened the door and shouted over his shoulder, "I've done what I can. Since you won't listen to reason, come to the fort so Superintendent Crozier can explain what a fool you are."

"Bien!" Dumont retorted as he shoved the man out of the doorway. "I will be most happy to discuss this with a man of principle."

McKay bristled, but Riel came out to stand beside them. "No, my friend," he said to Dumont. "You are needed here. We will send a message instead."

Dumont glowered. "I do not trust this company trader. How do you know he will give the message to the right man?"

McKay glared, and Riel took Dumont's arm and urged him back inside. "We will send two of our people with him," he promised. "Now let us find the words."

Red Eagle and Ben were on a bench beside the store listening. "Let's make ourselves scarce," Ben said. "I don't want to be picked to go back to the fort with McKay."

There was a shelter for hay in the corral behind Letendre's barn, and the two boys headed for it. When they were comfortably settled, Ben repeated almost word for word the discussion between Mitchell and Crozier. When he finished, Red Eagle was silent, his face serious.

Ben repeated his last words. "It doesn't look like the Mounted Police are about to give up the fort without a fight."

Red Eagle agreed. "You speak true. While you were away, I cleaned my rifle and sharpened my knife. I thought at last I can fight for my people, but I remember that Poundmaker has said though his heart is with Gabriel and all the Métis, we must make our lives better in our own way." The Cree paused, then said sadly, "I do not want to act against Poundmaker's wishes, but how can I turn away from you and Charity and all I have here?"

As he looked at his friend's troubled features, Ben tried to form the words to tell him about his own divided loyalties. Before he could say anything, though, he heard the boom of Dumont's voice nearby. "After Crozier reads the message from Riel, tell him this for me. Say Dumont respects him and wishes him well, for he is a fair man. Tell him that all who leave the fort will be given teams and provisions and a promise of safe passage to Fort Qu'Appelle. They have three days to decide what they will do."

Footsteps moved away, and Ben was about to make another attempt to explain his dilemma to Red Eagle when a voice spoke in his ear. He turned to see Dumont grinning at him from around the side of the lean-to. "*Bon nuit*. I wait for the report from my scout."

Ben tried to match the grin but failed. "I didn't hear much. I tried to stay out of my uncle's sight, but I stuck close to Hillyard and Crozier. The Mounted Police know you've been getting guns from some of the stores around here, and I expect Hillyard told you about the cannon." He thought for a moment, then said, "Oh, one more thing. They just got forty-three volunteers from Prince Albert."

Dumont's face suddenly sagged, and fatigue revealed itself in every line. "Your Tante Madeleine and Charity will be concerned, since we have sent no word. Before dark, return to the cabin and say that we are talking—nothing more. There is little for you to do here now but wait. I will send word when I need you."

The sun was low on the horizon when the two riders topped a rise in the trail and saw smoke from the Dumont cabin. The horses, smelling home and hay, broke into a gallop. Over his shoulder Red Eagle called, "Charity will be impatient to see you. Leave your horse and I will put it away with my own."

Ben didn't argue. He handed the reins to Red Eagle in front of the cabin and bounded to the step in front of the door. At the same moment it opened, and Tante Madeleine gave a cry of welcome. Ben hugged her, and she broke away to look behind him. "I'm sorry, Tante Madeleine. He couldn't get away just now, but he said not to worry. Everything's fine."

"Ben," Charity cried, reaching out as she moved toward the doorway. Tante Madeleine turned away, disappointment on her face.

"Hey, old sister of mine," Ben said, embracing her.

"Goodness," she said with a chuckle. "You must be as glad to see me as I am to see you."

It was so fine to be home that Ben couldn't think of a word for it. He surveyed the room with a smile. Everything was the same. No, not everything. On the table were long rolls of white strips. Ben's grin disappeared. They had been rolling bandages.

His eyes met Tante Madeleine's, and she shrugged. "One always needs plenty of those when spring arrives. If it is not a horse that has slipped on the ice, it is a child who has hurt his knees. We had nothing else to do."

Charity stood near the doorway, her head cocked as though listening. "Ben, where are Gabriel and Red Eagle? Are you alone?"

Red Eagle entered and said softly behind her, "I am here."

Charity's face lit up and she whirled with arms outstretched. The Cree caught her close to him, and over her head looked at Ben, who smiled. Just for a moment before he released her, Red Eagle gently touched Charity's hair.

NINE

The days passed quickly, for there were repairs to be made to the roof of the barn and cabin after the alternate freezing and thawing in early March. The warmer air brought violent gusts of wind, and Ben was grateful it was the top of the cabin they hammered on now instead of the tall house Dumont hadn't finished building. Their job completed, he followed Red Eagle down the ladder and helped him stow the tools and nails in a lean-to against the side of the cabin. "That's it then," he said.

Red Eagle darted a swift glance at Ben. "Your thoughts are the same as mine."

Ben nodded. "The three days they gave the Mounted Police to clear out passed yesterday. Gabriel said he'd send for us if there was trouble, but—"

"He sent us here to keep us from harm."

"I thought about that."

"I will go now and return tonight."

Ben shook his head. "No," he said, "we go together."

Red Eagle smiled and clapped his friend on the arm.

The Batoche settlement was quiet when they rode in, the only sounds the tinkle of a cowbell in a pasture upland from the river and the restless movements of the horses in the corral where Ben and Red Eagle left their mounts. For a heart-stopping moment Ben thought all the men had gone to attack Fort Carlton, but as they drew closer to Riel's headquarters, he heard voices—one of them Dumont's.

"Here are my sons," Dumont called out as Ben and Red Eagle opened the door. He left Riel at the map-covered table and came closer to peer at them anxiously. "All is well with Madeleine and Charity?"

Red Eagle nodded, and Ben said, "Sure, the hens are laying again and we fixed the roof and the fence around the barn." He tried to be casual. "We thought we'd ride over and see if you need us for anything."

Dumont considered this, then shook his head. "No, for we have no word from the fort and it was decided to give them more time. If there is trouble, I will need you for a most important—"

A man burst into the room, his eyes wide. He gasped for breath as he spit out his words. "Gabriel! Just now I saw many of Crozier's men across the river."

The big Métis rushed to the door. "Where, Patrice? Downriver? Upriver? Where?"

"Are they coming? Are they coming?" Riel screamed, snatching his wooden cross from the table.

The tired man dropped into a chair. "I do not know. I only know they march west."

Dumont leaned over him. "Think now, Patrice. What distance from the river and how many? Did they see you?"

Patrice, calmer now, thought before he answered. "Maybe seven miles north of the river, and two dozen men." He shrugged. "Maybe they saw me, but they did not give me a polite salute."

Dumont looked at Riel, who was seated again. "It is a puzzle. They would not come so near to us if they were marching to Prince Albert."

Riel's eyes shone. "St. Laurent! They will attack St. Laurent."

Dumont turned to stare through the small window. "No, they march nowhere except to show us they are not afraid and can do as they please."

Riel bit his lip. "Then we have their answer."

"We cannot be certain," Dumont said. "We should wait a few more days, though I think Crozier knows we must gather more arms and ammunition."

"And he will know the stores at Duck Lake have guns," Red Eagle said.

Dumont nodded, then a slow grin spread across his face. "Red Eagle, you would make a good general. Go up and ring the bell to summon the men. And you, Ben, bring the horses and wagon."

Sometime after, in Duck Lake, Ben counted thirty men in all emptying the three stores of their weapons. Dumont apologized to an angry Hillyard Mitchell, who watched the Métis loot his store. "We take only guns and ammunition. Later, we will pay a fair price, but for now we must keep what we have." When Mitchell turned away without replying, Dumont added, "Truly I am sorry. You have been our friend."

Mitchell scratched his head, then said, "I still am, so I should tell you that the Mounted Police figured on getting to my stock of guns ahead of you. I expect they're on their way right now."

Dumont's face cleared, and his eyes began to shine. "Load faster, my friends! We may have guests before dark."

With Ben's wagon full, he and Red Eagle were ordered back to Batoche with the load. One man accompanied them with instructions to alert the rest of the Métis fighting men, but the two boys were not to return.

"I shoot well," Red Eagle protested. "Ben, too."

Dumont clasped Red Eagle's shoulders. "I know that. Do

not forget. I have hunted with you. But I have a better use for the two of you. I will tell you what that is in the morning."

Ben and Red Eagle had the headquarters house in Batoche to themselves. Riel's wife and children were staying with another family, and Riel and Dumont were at Duck Lake. Ben tossed restlessly on the floor in the office. It smelled of pine and reminded him of the cabin on the Red River where he had lived long before he was caught up in this nightmare. He uttered a whispered prayer: "Help me to do what's right and, most of all, please don't let harm come to Tante Madeleine or Charity or Gabriel Dumont or my friend, Red Eagle."

The next morning men arrived in bunches to meet and trade information down by the Batoche ferry landing. A good many of them, Ben noted, were English-speaking Métis from around Prince Albert. Although he and Red Eagle were impatient to hear the latest rumours, they obeyed their stomachs and followed their noses to a small cabin not far from headquarters where the women prepared food for the men who didn't live in Batoche.

Ben and Red Eagle ate the bannock, rabbit, and potatoes fried with onions heartily. When they finished, they returned to headquarters to wait. The noon hour passed and still there was no word from Riel or Dumont. Rumours of the arrival of hordes of Mounted Police flew about the village, but hardly anyone took them seriously until a horse plunged across the ice-filled river while the rider waved his arms and shouted unintelligible words. Ben and Red Eagle reached the ferry landing to hear him rasp, "Twenty-two men from Fort Carlton left for Duck Lake before dawn!"

Ben's heart missed a beat, but the men on the landing looked at one another and laughed. "Twenty-two men!" one of them said. "Dumont has thirty, which is twice what he'll need to take care of those policemen." The man hooked his thumbs in the wide blue sash he wore around his middle. "Still, it might be interesting to see what's happening. Let's ride to Duck Lake."

Red Eagle and Ben looked at each other and sprinted for their horses. Side by side, they rode in the middle of a seemingly endless string of men riding two abreast. The trail dipped through coulees and brushed against trees as it wound between the two branches of the Saskatchewan River. Despite the roughness of the terrain, it took less than an hour to reach Duck Lake. Ben had expected to hear gunfire, but heard only the murmur of voices as they drew closer. Two men stepped from the bushes on each side of the trail with rifles over their shoulders, their faces wreathed in smiles. "Too bad for you to be so late," they jeered good-naturedly. "It is over without firing a shot."

A chorus of "What happened?" brought a response from the other man.

"Crozier only sent fifteen of his men. The rest were clerks from Prince Albert who wanted to rescue the guns and shot from the stores before the bad men of Batoche could steal them."

There was a roar of laughter from the new arrivals, and the first man added, "The shots fired came from the mouths. Back and forth with Gabriel Dumont winning. McKay thought to teach him a lesson, but when he took hold of our general he found it was himself who ended up on the ground."

Dumont appeared suddenly from the trees, grinning and trading jokes as he reached up to shake hands with some of the newcomers. The column dissolved into a crowd, each man eager to hear the news. Dumont said, "I am grateful you are here. Our first meeting with the enemy was a joke, but they will return, and soon. We have made an outpost here and you who are captains must gather your men. You will be quick with this and report to me at Hillyard's store."

Ben thought Dumont hadn't noticed they were in the

crowd until the men began to disperse. Frowning, the Métis leader looked first at Red Eagle, then at Ben. "Strange, I do not recall inviting you to this party."

Ben coughed uneasily as he and Red Eagle waited in silence for the scolding that was sure to come. He sighed inwardly with relief when Dumont's face brightened.

"Since you are here, I must make use of you. With the speed of a rabbit, go about our camp and count the men. Report to me at the store when you are done."

It wasn't an easy task, for the men moved around and Ben was worried they might have counted some of them twice. But they told Dumont there were about two hundred Métis, plus a sprinkling of Cree and Assiniboine who had slipped in and out of the brush so quickly they couldn't be sure of their number.

"Très bien!" Dumont said when they finished their report. He stood beside Riel in front of the store, feet apart, hands on hips, eyeing the half circle of captains in front of him. "Let them hide behind their cannon. We have plenty of men for what comes."

"You are sure they will come?" Riel asked.

"Superintendent Crozier has great pride in his police force. After he learns that his men retreated quickly this morning, he will return to fight to keep its honour."

Before Riel could respond further, hoof beats drummed into the tiny settlement and a rider pulled his horse to a sliding stop. "Gabriel, you were right! Crozier has brought all his men—maybe sixty, with forty volunteers. They are six miles away and they have a cannon."

Riel waved his crucifix. "Come, men," he cried, "the battle is here!"

"Louis," Dumont snapped, "the battle is not here. We must proceed with haste. The rest will stay here while I take twenty-five men to a hill two miles ahead. It looks over the road and has plenty of cover, which will be good for us." He pointed to one of the captains. "On one side a trail goes down to a cabin hidden in the trees. The enemy may try to occupy it to surprise us. Get there fast with your men." Two of the other captains were ordered to ride ahead with their men to opposite ends of a shallow ravine that paralleled the road below the hill. Once there, they were to position their men to catch the enemy in a crossfire. As the captains turned to go, Dumont cautioned them. "Dead men are useless, but many prisoners may encourage Dewdney and Macdonald to bargain with us."

Unbidden, Red Eagle and Ben followed the men led by Dumont. No one spoke as they rode until they emerged from the sparse forest onto a narrow, grassy plateau. The forest continued downward on both sides of the clearing. Ahead, it ended abruptly in a short, steep slope with a shallow ravine at the bottom that separated the hill from the wide trail.

Dumont signalled a halt, then quickly ordered some of his men to spread themselves in the long ravine and on the brow of the hill. At the bottom of the slope, hidden behind the giant roots of a fallen cottonwood, Ben watched. He turned to whisper to Red Eagle, who had moved away to stare through the trees. "Wait here," the Cree said, then disappeared.

Long moments passed before Red Eagle reappeared, bent double as he scurried up the hill where Dumont lay prone, his rifle pointed downward at the trail as it emerged from the trees. Ben couldn't stand waiting and followed in a running crouch. He met his friend coming back, and they stopped to lie side by side as Red Eagle explained why he had left. "I heard a sound and saw a police scout. I followed him and watched from behind a tree across the trail. They know we are here, for they turned their wagons on their sides in the trees to make a barricade. It will be a hard fight, Ben. I saw the big gun."

"What did Gabriel say?"

"He said, *'Très bien,'* but I do not know what is good about any of this. His ambush is useless now. They must parley."

From the top of the hill a white flag waved, and moments later one appeared in the distance at the edge of a stand of trees. On the hill Ben saw one of the captains, Dumont's brother, Isidore, wave his hands as his words floated down. "It must not be you, Gabriel. They know if you are killed the men will no longer fight. For that reason they may be tempted to shoot you."

"Crozier would not allow his men to kill the bearer of a white flag."

"No, he would not," Isidore agreed, "but remember, he has volunteers who are not accustomed to the rules of battle, and some may be without honour. I would be as worthless to them dead as I am alive. Let me speak for you."

Riel and the other captain urged him to agree, and Dumont sighed. "Very well. Take one other man."

Isidore grinned. "I choose Aseeweyin."

"You are wise," Dumont said with a fleeting smile. "He is old and half blind, but he is a legend among the Cree for his bravery in battle when he was young."

Isidore slipped back behind the hill to the trees where the horses were tied and reappeared mounted. The rider beside him looked small and shrunken under his long white-feathered headdress, but as they drew closer, Ben saw the Indian's head lift proudly as he gripped his rifle firmly. The two riders circled through the trees around the hill, Isidore carrying the white flag as they rode to meet the two men coming toward them. One was a uniformed policeman, the other probably an interpreter.

The tall palomino ridden by Aseeweyin grew restive as the men talked. Even though the Cree used pressure with both hands and feet to still the horse, the animal danced playfully. It wasn't right for an old war chief to have trouble with his mount, and Aseeweyin's face wore a determined expression as he spoke to it. For Ben, what followed happened with excruciating slowness: the restless horse, the rifle Aseeweyin awkwardly brought up to shift to his other hand while he reached down for the animal's ears, the policeman opposite him who ducked back as though threatened.

When the shot rang out, Isidore Dumont fell from his horse, the white flag clutched in his hand.

The hill erupted in sound as Riel shouted, "Answer their fire!" Over the thunder of guns Ben felt, more than heard, the anguished roar from Dumont's throat as he struggled with the men who prevented him from running to his brother. Ben was sick with horror. Aseeweyin's horse had bolted with him clinging to its mane, but there was no doubt Isidore was dead.

When Red Eagle tugged his arm, Ben turned and slipped into the trees to wait for a chance to join Dumont. Total confusion reigned. He watched from behind a clump of aspens, but Red Eagle had a better vantage point behind a rock closer to the open slope of the hill. "Many of our men have fallen," the Cree boy reported over his shoulder. "I think they are trying to move down the hill, but the cannon scatters too much shot."

Something about the cannon nagged at Ben. He had been allowed to help fire it on the queen's birthday. Shouting to Red Eagle that he would be right back, Ben went into the trees and made a wide circle behind the barricaded policemen. He didn't have a plan, but he had to do something.

Boldly he strode up a narrow path toward the enemy. "Who are you?" a sentry demanded, stepping from behind a tree to press the muzzle of his rifle against Ben's chest.

Ben backed up, raised his hands, and scowled to hide his fear. "Watch that," he said crossly. "I got a message from the fort for Superintendent Crozier."

He was ready with an answer if the man insisted he give the message to him, but it wasn't needed. The sentry examined Ben's face, then stepped aside. "Right, I seen you around the fort. Go on ahead. Crozier's over there." He gestured to his right with his thumb. "But unless you got good news for him, you better give him the message and get goin' again."

"Why's that?"

"He's walkin' about four feet off the ground and cussin' with every step because that interpreter killed one of the fellas carryin' the white flag and started this shootin' match. We didn't have a chance to get set, so now they got us outnumbered and outflanked and all we got for cover are the wagons we turned over."

"Sure wish he hadn't shot that man."

"Me, too. War's a nasty business. I guess the interpreter was a mite nervous, and when the Indian moved his rifle, he figured he was takin' aim right at him. Like I said, watch yourself."

Ben nodded his thanks and walked away briskly. He checked over his shoulder to make certain the sentry wasn't watching before he ducked into the trees to avoid Crozier. Then he headed for the big gun tucked back in the bushes. A plan formed in his head when he saw one of the casually dressed volunteers roll a small keg from a wagon.

"I been sent to relieve you," Ben said. "This is heavy work. You get to rest for a half hour, but don't get back late."

"Sure," the man said. "I'm more'n glad of that. I been wonderin' why I got in this at all. Haulin' powder and shot ain't my idea of fightin' a battle."

"How's it going?"

"They got us caught in a crossfire, and the sergeant says they got us outnumbered ten to one. But they can't get close enough to do anything about it as long as we got the big gun to blast away." He gestured in the direction of a thicket about ten yards off. A tangle of willow and wild rosebushes bare of leaves but nestled among stubby, half-grown spruce trees, it effectively screened the cannon from view.

Ben clenched his jaw as the gun spoke with a mighty roar. In the distance he heard a shrill scream. "Heavier than I thought it'd be," he said, grunting as he hoisted the small barrel to his shoulder.

The volunteer nodded. "That'd be the shot. Lead's heavy. Powder barrels don't weigh on you so much. Now you take these newfangled repeatin' rifles..."

The voice droned on, but Ben barely heard. His heart

thumped and he ran his tongue over dry lips as he tried to come up with a plan to destroy the cannon. If he couldn't do that, the next best thing would be to light a fire in the powder wagon. But it wasn't likely he could do that without being seen, for the man showed no sign of going anywhere to rest. He was still talking when Ben headed down the path.

Two men were with the cannon—one to pour in powder and shot and the other to aim and fire. Ben placed the barrel on the ground carefully, and the gunner looked at Ben with approval. "First time one of you volunteers got sense enough to handle these with some care. Now pry open the lid and hurry up with another keg of powder. I'm runnin' low."

Ben snatched up a pry bar lying on the ground and knelt to pop the lid off the barrel. It almost tipped over and spilled the lead balls. "Step smartly now," the loader snapped. "We need that powder, too."

As Ben straightened, his heart raced. He had found a plan to put the gun out of action. The gunner spoke to him twice before he heard. "I said you don't have to hurry *that* much." He patted the back of the cannon. "Old Thumper here's got to rest a few minutes, anyway. She's pretty hot."

The memory of the day the seven-pounder had been fired at the fort for a visiting party of Hudson's Bay officers flashed through Ben's mind. Uncle Lawrence had clucked over the man loading the cannon, telling him to put in the powder before the shot else the results would be disastrous. But how? How could he...? Ben's mind cleared. Taking a deep breath, he turned to the gunner and loader and raised a hand in farewell. As he backed away, his foot collided with the barrel of shot. It rolled onto its side, scattering balls over the frozen ground around the bushes.

"You blasted fool!" the loader shouted, lunging forward, fist clenched.

Ben ducked back. "I'm sorry," he said, the tremor in his voice only half pretence. "I'll pick them up. I'll find all of them."

The gunner, clearly the one in charge, grabbed the loader by the arm before he could strike Ben. He took a deep breath and blew it out noisily. "You do that, lad, and be quick about it. We'll be just over there grabbing a smoke. When we get back, I want to find all the shot in the keg and no dirt. You hear me?"

Ben worked swiftly, scarcely able to believe his luck. Shielded by the gun, he scooped up double handfuls of shot and dropped them into the cannon barrel. Four times he did so, with one eye on the two men leaning against a tree a few feet away. Hoping fervently that would be enough to damage the gun, Ben turned his attention to the rest of the lead balls scattered on the ground and managed to gather enough to half fill the wooden container before the two men returned.

"That all you found?" the loader asked, peering at the keg.

"I'm still looking," Ben replied. He moved over the ground on his knees to search under a rosebush. "They're hard to spot."

"The fight won't wait. Go get another one and the powder." As Ben rose, the loader added, "You're as dumb as a year-old sheep."

"Mighty dumb," Ben agreed. He waved a hand. "I'll go get some more."

When he passed the sentry, the cannon spoke with a muffled roar, and Ben allowed himself to smile.

TEN

Ducking low, Ben weaved through the thickly branched spruce trees, thankful for the carpet of needles that deadened his footsteps. When he heard fewer rifles cracking and more muskets booming, he knew he had reached his own lines. He paused to search the woods for a possible Métis sentry. Then, without warning, a hand was clamped over his mouth and a voice whispered in his ear, "Get down."

Ben dropped to the ground and stretched out on his belly. He had recognized the voice, and turned to look at Red Eagle beside him. "What's the idea? Is this some kind of joke?"

Red Eagle shook his head slowly. "There is no time for jokes. If someone saw you run to the other side, it is better they not see you again before we reach Gabriel."

Ben was shocked. "I didn't run. I went to take care of that blasted cannon."

"I know. When it no longer fired, I told myself Ben has done well."

"Does Gabriel know?"

"Come. We will tell him."

Following Red Eagle's lead, Ben circled upward through the trees to emerge on the hill well behind the line of Métis firing at Crozier and his men. It was a bewildering sight: horses struggled wildly as they tried to get loose from their tethers, and men darted in and out of the fir trees covering the sides of the hill. At the edge of the trees Ben paused to look down at two blanket-draped bodies.

"Think one of them's Isidore?"

Red Eagle shook his head. "He lies on the field still. Gabriel tried to get him, but the men held him back, or he would have been killed, as well."

Something twisted in Ben's chest, and he turned away to survey the men on their stomachs as they fired from the brow of the hill. "Where's Gabriel? I don't see him over there."

"Perhaps he is in the ravine now. There is a way to it over here." Ben followed his friend down into the woods again, bending double until they slid into the shallow ravine. Two men, crouched with rifles pointed through the trees, turned their heads to grin at them. Ben knew they were sharpshooters placed there by Dumont to discourage any attempt to circle around the Métis on the hill. Red Eagle and Ben bent lower as they left the shelter of the woods and crept through the middle of the ravine below the hill. Tilting his head, Ben glanced upward and saw the barrels of Métis muskets spitting a deadly warning to any policeman who dared to show himself from the trees on the other side of the trail.

In the damp and icy gully men knelt less than six feet apart. Their shots were less frequent now, and they took careful aim before they squeezed the triggers on their long-barrelled weapons. Over the spasmodic crack of gunfire, Ben could hear men down the line call to one another good-naturedly as though they were at a fair. "Ho there, Patrice, your aim is not so good today. Too much wine, eh?"

"And my advice to you, my friend, is to put powder in your gun. It makes the ball fly faster."

"Gabriel is up there," Red Eagle called over his shoulder. The two boys quickened their pace, almost on hands and knees now, for the gully had become increasingly shallow. A jumble of boulders on the edge of the trail ahead gave extra protection. Here, they found Dumont shouting encouragement to his men each time he thrust Le Petit over a rock and fired. Beside him, the musket of a man Ben recognized as their neighbour, Baptiste Vanda, spat angrily.

Red Eagle touched Ben's arm. "We must wait until he reloads."

Almost as Red Eagle spoke, Dumont paused to fumble for shells in his pocket. Frowning as he searched, he straightened for an instant almost to his full height. In that moment a bullet found its mark.

Ben heard a voice cry Dumont's name, unaware it was his own. Beside Red Eagle, he darted out of the ravine to reach the fallen man. Together they turned him over. Blood oozed from a long gash on one side of his head, and his eyes were closed. "Gabriel," Ben whispered, "please, Gabriel."

Red Eagle pressed his ear against the big man's chest. "His heart beats. He is alive."

"I have one big headache," Dumont said without opening his eyes. "Which is nothing compared to what I will do to you. Did I not say you were to stay back with the horses?"

Before they could reply Edouard Dumont pushed them aside and bent over his brother. "Gabriel, how bad is it? You are bleeding from the head."

"It is only a scratch." Dumont frowned. "Edouard, why are you here? Have you forgotten the rules of the hunt? When I fall, you must take command."

"But, Gabriel, I must—"

Dumont opened his eyes. "What you must do is rally the men. Tell them I did not die, and I will not. Now go."

With a glance at Ben that said to look after his brother, Edouard zigzagged back up the hill. Dumont closed his eyes for a moment, then opened them to look at the rifle by his side. He picked it up and held it out to Red Eagle. "Hand it up to Baptiste Vanda," he ordered. "Le Petit has the range two times the musket he shoots."

Vanda fired in rapid succession to cover Dumont's sliding descent from the edge of the road. With the help of Ben and Red Eagle, he lay against the side of the ravine in a half-sitting position and closed his eyes. Ben gently parted Dumont's thick, dark hair with his fingers and found the long gash. The blood oozed more slowly now, but it needed attention. "Wish we had some water," he muttered. "And I wish Tante Madeleine could tell me what to do."

Red Eagle turned away. "I will find water."

Less than a minute later Ben heard the dull thud of a bullet, along with a sharp cry. It was followed by a low moan.

"Red Eagle!" Ben cried.

ELEVEN

Ben gasped with relief when Red Eagle appeared, holding out a canteen. “Laframboise was hit, but he lives.” The Cree’s eyes told Ben the wound was serious.

“Auguste,” Dumont called. His face was twisted in anguish as he swayed to his knees. With each boy holding an arm, he lurched through the ravine until he reached the side of his cousin. Laframboise lay against the side of the gully, clutching his blood-soaked sleeve. His face was a waxy grey and sweat beaded his forehead. “Ah, Auguste, I am thankful the bullet found your arm and not your leg else all the ladies might have blamed me if your dancing had been spoiled.”

“You must dance with them for me, Gabriel,” Laframboise said, slumping forward.

Ben leaned over and raised the dead man’s arm. There was a hole on both sides of his sleeve, and in the jacket that covered his ribs.

Dumont's cry was full of pain and rage. "Help me up. I will avenge the death of my brother and cousin."

"Listen!" a voice yelled. "The police have stopped firing."

Dumont closed his eyes for a moment, then said, "Stay where you are and wait." To Red Eagle, he added, "Go to Edouard and learn what is happening."

The Cree boy returned quickly. "The Mounted Police are retreating. Your brother wishes to follow, but Riel will not allow it."

"When we have them on the run?" Dumont got to his feet unsteadily. With the help of the two boys he climbed from the ditch and staggered up the slope.

Men still lined the hilltop, their muskets and rifles ready, but the rest of the fighting Métis and Indians crowded around a wagon where Riel waved his crucifix. Heads turned and a cheer rose when they saw Dumont. Riel jumped from the wagon, and the men made a path for him as he strode forward. Edouard reached his brother first. "Gabriel, if we follow, we can capture our enemies," he cried.

Riel spoke firmly. "Gabriel, there has been enough killing. We must return now to Batoche."

Dumont frowned. "Why did we fight then? A battle is not the same as making a cup of tea, Louis. We do not stop because we are afraid to become too strong."

"I tell you, my general, all I know is this—it is our Lord's wish. He watches and the world watches what we do here. He knows and they will know we only defend what is ours by right. We are not aggressors. We are defenders."

Conflicting emotions flickered in Dumont's eyes as he stared back at Riel. Then his shoulders slumped. "Very well. I cannot argue against the will of God." He turned his back on Riel to give orders to his men.

Ben and Red Eagle were part of the dozen men detailed to find any weapons or ammunition the enemy may have left behind. Together they went to get their horses, which were tethered with the others in the trees. When they were mounted, they rode directly to the clearing in the bushes from where the cannon had sprayed its painful message over the men who had defended the hill. The big gun had disappeared but, dismounting, Ben searched the area, anyway. A dozen feet from where the cannon had made furrows in the hard earth he found a round chunk of iron the size of his head. Engraved on it was: PROPERTY OF NWMP.

The detail returned through the woods to the back of the hill with five wagons, eight horses, and twelve rifles with a dozen boxes of ammunition for each. Dumont scarcely seemed to notice as he strode back and forth in front of a half-dozen prisoners. "You killed my brother under a white flag," he raged, "and my cousin who was like a brother to me. Why should I not kill you?"

The men, all Prince Albert volunteers, listened white-faced and silent, but they stood shoulder to shoulder with heads held high and displayed no fear. Perhaps that was what saved them, or maybe it was Edouard's report that they had found the bodies of twelve volunteers lying in the woods. Whatever it was, Ben was relieved to see the fury disappear from Dumont's eyes and hear him speak quietly to the prisoners. "So, such is war, *n'est-ce pas*?" To Edouard he said, "Put the bodies into the cabin by the ravine." Nodding toward the prisoners, he added, "And send one of these men to Prince Albert with a message that those who wish to may come in safety to get their dead."

"And the rest of the prisoners?" Edouard asked.

"Take them to Batoche and put them in a house with the others."

The Métis fighters drifted away, but their angry muttering testified to the disappointment they felt with Riel's decision not to pursue the enemy. The horses and rifles they gained did little to compensate for the loss of five comrades. When Riel and Dumont were alone, Ben moved forward with outstretched hands.

"So," Dumont said, slowly turning over the chunk of metal

Ben had given him. "You found this on the battlefield?"

Ben nodded. "I'm pretty certain it's a piece from the seven-pounder." His own feelings were mixed. He wanted to believe spiking the cannon would make up for doing his uncle's bidding, but did it?

"Ben found a way to destroy the cannon," Red Eagle said. His words were spoken casually, but his grin and shining eyes betrayed his pride in his friend.

Dumont's bushy eyebrows shot up. "Tell me."

In a few short sentences Ben explained, and when he finished, Dumont turned to Riel with a sour smile. "And this is the young boy you did not trust."

Ben suddenly felt cold. Had his conversations with his uncle been overheard?

If they had, Riel didn't let on. Instead, he shrugged and said, "If I have been suspicious, it was only because my man at the fort saw him talk with Lawrence Clarke."

"Clarke is his uncle. What do you expect? It is not Ben's fault. No one can select his uncles." Dumont grasped Ben's shoulders and hugged him. "Now you are my son." He stepped back and sternly regarded the two boys in turn. "And sons must obey. You are to stay far back from the fighting. We do not know how this will end. You, Ben, must not be seen by our enemies, for it is possible one day you will live among them again and they would make trouble for you."

Red Eagle and Ben said nothing, and Dumont frowned. "Is that understood?"

When the two boys nodded slowly, his face relaxed. Ignoring Riel, he placed a big hand on the shoulder of each boy and carefully trudged toward the horses. "Come, we go home. Tante Madeleine and Charity will be concerned."

With one hand Red Eagle shaded his eyes from the sun as he stared into the distance. "Tante Madeleine does not wait."

As her horse galloped toward them, Tante Madeleine cried out, "Gabriel, you are wounded!"

Ben snatched the bridle of the lathered horse, and its rider slid to the ground. She trembled visibly as Dumont held her close and stroked her hair. "It is nothing, my treasure." After a moment he released her and stood back. "Bad news flies swifter than I thought possible."

"I did not need to be told," she said. "I knew."

Tante Madeleine had brought bandages and medicines and, as she cleaned Dumont's wound, she answered Ben's anxious question. "Charity is not alone. Father André stopped by on his way to Saskatoon and waits with her, but she is very worried about you."

"Go then, the two of you," Dumont ordered. "We will follow when this mother hen is satisfied there is no more clucking to do over my head."

As Ben and Red Eagle neared the Dumonts' cabin, the door opened and Charity appeared. With Ben's shout of "We're home!" she darted from the doorway and onto a patch of ice. Red Eagle flung himself from his still-running horse and helped Charity to her feet almost before she hit the ground. She leaned against him and giggled as she smoothed her long skirts.

"Goodness me," she said. "That must have been a sight to make anyone laugh." When she brushed her hair away from her face with both hands, Ben saw they were badly skinned, but said nothing. She was embarrassed enough.

Father André emerged from the cabin and hurried toward them. "Ben, what happened at Duck Lake?"

"There was a fight with the Mounted Police. Gabriel was grazed by a bullet, but he's all right now. Tante Madeleine is taking care of him."

Father André spoke so softly that Ben barely heard the question. "And the result of this fight?"

Suddenly Ben felt very tired and hungry. He took his sister's arm. "Charity got her hands a mite dirty and wants to go inside and wash. Red Eagle can tell you all about it."

In the kitchen Ben made himself stand quietly and watch as Charity dipped water from a pail into a tin basin. She winced a little as she plunged in her hands, then reached for the soap. "Tell me about the fight," she demanded abruptly. "And, Ben, please don't try to spare me. Is it true Gabriel will be all right?"

"It's true," Ben said with as much conviction as he could muster. "He's walking around and giving orders same as always. But his brother, Isidore, was killed. Do you remember him?"

"Oh, Ben," Charity wailed, "he has a wife and children and I liked him."

"There's more."

When he finished, Charity grasped his arm. "You and Red Eagle shouldn't have been there. You might have been killed, too." It was then that Ben told her about spiking the cannon.

"Ben, promise you'll never do anything so foolish again. When Tante Madeleine hears of it, she'll make certain you're right here if there's another battle."

"I had to do something, Charity. More'n likely Uncle Lawrence made up that story about the police coming to arrest the council, and if I hadn't repeated it to Gabriel, maybe he wouldn't have gone after the guns in Duck Lake. I did what Uncle Lawrence said I should and look what happened. Men died because of me."

"Don't be foolish, Ben. This trouble started months before we came here. It's the fault of the government for not even pretending to listen to the people. You tried to help."

"I try to tell myself the same thing, and sometimes I almost believe it," Ben admitted. "But there's one thing nothing can change. I spied for Uncle Lawrence, and there's nothing skunkier than spying on your friends."

Just then there was a soft sound behind him, and Ben whirled. Red Eagle stood in the doorway.

TWELVE

As Red Eagle stared, Ben struggled for words. "Listen—" he began.

"We will talk later," Red Eagle broke in. "The priest wishes to say goodbye."

Ben's heart was a lump of ice, and he felt Charity tremble as they walked to the cabin door. Father André looked down from his horse. "I have a long journey to make, but first I will go to Duck Lake. There are those who need the sacrament." He made the sign of the cross in the air. "May God bless the three of you." His horse began a fast walk and then a canter.

"Come," Red Eagle said quietly, "we will talk."

Charity stepped inside and felt her way to the long table. She slid onto a bench, hands clasped tightly in front of her. "Please, Red Eagle," she said, "Ben has been so troubled not knowing right from wrong, but he—"

Ben touched her shoulder, and she fell silent. "It's best this way, Charity. I been wanting to tell Red Eagle for a long time. It's a relief to be straight with him."

"You spied for our enemies," Red Eagle said flatly. "Lawrence Clarke made you do this. How?"

"I now know how stupid I been. The way Uncle Lawrence put it, I thought I was helping to keep things peaceful here. Deep down I think I knew better, but I wanted to believe..." Ben shook his head and stared out the window. "Seems like everything I did turned out wrong."

The corners of Red Eagle's mouth turned up. "You spiked the gun. That did not turn out wrong."

"That made me feel a bit better, but not enough."

"Please, Red Eagle," Charity pleaded, "make Ben stop blaming himself."

"Charity is right, Ben. I heard when you told her you were the one to speak of the police Clarke said would come to Batoche, but you are wrong. Riel has two who spy for him in the fort. One brought the same tale to Riel, even as you told Gabriel here in the cabin."

"Oh, Ben," Charity cried. "Do you understand? Everything would have happened the same way even if we had never come to Gabriel's Crossing."

Ben's shoulders felt lighter, and he smiled weakly, then became serious again. "But there's no changing when Uncle Lawrence told me to spy. I didn't come right out and say no."

Red Eagle crossed the room and sat on the bench beside Charity. His face was expressionless as he studied Ben. "What have you told him?"

"I been trying to remember. The first time was when I told him about Mr. Forget meeting with Gabriel at Vanda's house." Red Eagle shrugged, and Ben nodded. "He'd already heard about it. Then I told my uncle about Riel's idea to take the government's money and use it to start a newspaper. Worst of all, I told him Gabriel and his friends signed an oath to fight if they had to. After that he did get a few extra police at Fort Carlton."

"Oh, Ben," Charity interrupted. "Even while we were at the fort everyone knew Uncle Lawrence sent telegrams to Ottawa to tell them the Métis were ready to fight, and the reserve Indians, too."

Ben patted his sister's shoulder. "It's not the same, Charity. They likely never paid attention to his warnings then."

"And if he sent word to Ottawa an oath had been signed, are you so sure they would heed his warning now?" Red Eagle asked. When Ben didn't answer, he continued. "And what else, Ben? Does Clarke know Gabriel asked the Cree and Assiniboine to join our battle?"

Ben shook his head. "I don't know. I never said anything about Gabriel going around to the reserves, and he didn't ask."

Red Eagle smiled. "Ben, I think you make a very bad spy."

"It feels good to get it off my chest. I wanted to tell you and Tante Madeleine a long while ago."

"Ben," Charity said sharply, "you mustn't say a word about this to Tante Madeleine or Gabriel either until all this is over. They have enough to worry about, and you don't have the right to make yourself feel better by telling them something that might hurt them."

"Charity is right, Ben," Red Eagle said. "It is—" He stopped suddenly and listened.

Ben heard it, too: the creak of wagon wheels and the steady thump of hoofs against frozen ground. He rose and flung open the door. Outlined against the setting sun, Tante Madeleine sat on the wagon seat, the reins firmly in her hands, her husband beside her. Their horses followed behind. Charity waited in the doorway while Red Eagle darted forward to hold the team and Ben helped Dumont to the ground. The tired general rubbed his backside with both hands and grimaced. "Had I been better acquainted with the seat of Monsieur Cardinal's wagon, I would have stayed on my horse."

"Then why did you not use the bed of robes I made in the

back of the wagon?" Tante Madeleine asked over her shoulder as she tossed the reins to Red Eagle and climbed over the wheel.

"A bed for a man who returns from a victory?" Dumont scoffed. "I cannot believe you would expect that of me."

Tante Madeleine wasn't impressed. "Help him inside, Ben. His wound has to be dressed again and he must sleep."

Dumont didn't protest, and leaned heavily on Ben as they made their way inside the cabin. He paused only long enough to receive a welcoming hug from Charity before they proceeded to the curtained alcove and his waiting bed.

The next afternoon Ben and Red Eagle watched as Tante Madeleine carefully removed the bandage from her husband's head. The bullet had grazed one side near the top, leaving a furrow that neatly parted his hair. She seemed satisfied as she cleaned the wound and paid little attention to Dumont's grumbling. "It is nothing," he said. "A scratch only."

Charity stood nearby, her expression anxious. Red Eagle went to her side and said, "Do not be concerned, Charity. His wound is more than a scratch, but it heals well."

Tante Madeleine's lips twisted into a wry smile. "That is true, and those who are sick from a wound cannot devour so much food as this one has today."

Dumont's face assumed an expression of indignation, but the retort forming on his lips was stilled as the clatter of hoof beats filtered into the cabin. The door flew open, and Edouard Dumont burst into the room. His words came out in short gasps as though he had been running.

"Gabriel, we have learned that Commissioner Irvine of the Mounted Police in Winnipeg arrived at Fort Carlton last night with eighty-three men. Superintendent Crozier is in trouble because he did not wait for him to help fight us."

Dumont hooted with laughter. "He is fortunate, this Irvine, else he, too, would have tasted the vinegar of defeat at the hands of the Métis."

"There is more. This Commissioner Irvine believes we will

attack the fort for weapons, and Prince Albert, as well, thus it has been decided to abandon Fort Carlton and take everything to defend Prince Albert."

Dumont nodded a grudging approval. "A good decision. Carlton is only a Hudson's Bay post and impossible to defend, but Ottawa would regard Prince Albert as important." His expression hardened. "When do they leave Fort Carlton?"

"They load the wagons even as we speak. The men have been ordered to take anything they can carry, even that which belongs to the company. The rest they will sink below the ice. Nothing is to be left that would be of use to us."

Dumont rose and paced the long room. "It is too late then to gather the men to stop them at the gates of the fort itself, but with horses laden it will take a day and a half for them to reach Prince Albert. In that time much can happen."

He whirled suddenly, eyes bright. "Edouard, do you remember the coulee where you shot the white wolf in the winter two years ago?"

His brother nodded. "Five, maybe six miles downriver from the fort. A good place for an ambush."

"Send word to meet in our headquarters at first light. We will need less than a hundred men, and only those with rifles."

As Edouard jerked open the door and left the cabin, Tante Madeleine turned to Dumont, fists on her hips, eyes blazing. "Are you mad, Gabriel? We have the men who died in the battle to bury tomorrow and wounded men who must be treated. And you are not yet fit to lead men in a fight."

"Then I must not use what strength I have to fight first with my wife," Dumont said softly, steel in his voice.

Tante Madeleine turned away. Charity's head moved toward the sound of her retreating footsteps and rose to follow them into the kitchen.

Dumont glanced at the two boys. "This time you must not come. I want you to stay and look after our home. Red Eagle, you will saddle a fresh horse for me, and you, Ben, will see that Tante Madeleine does not punish me by neglecting to place in the saddlebags my tin cup and plate with my food." He smiled, but his eyes were unhappy.

"She's worried, Gabriel," Ben said. "You do look sort of peaked."

Dumont grasped Ben's hand. "My friend, we have concerns more important than a headache. We are few and poorly armed and must seize each opportunity that presents itself."

Outside, the horse waited, saddlebags bulging. There were only goodbyes to be said. Dumont swiftly hugged Red Eagle and Ben and kissed Charity. His wife stared at him for a long moment, then reached out her hands. Dumont held her close and stroked her hair before he opened the door.

Louis Riel was on the doorstep, one hand upraised as though ready to knock. Behind him stood a disgusted Edouard Dumont.

Wordlessly Dumont motioned to the table. When the two men were seated, he sat on a bench opposite them. "We met on the trail," Edouard explained. "Louis does not want me to assemble the men."

Riel clasped his hands in front of him and stared at Dumont with pleading eyes. "Please, my general, hear what I have to say and you will forgive me once again if I seem to countermand your orders."

Dumont said nothing and the other man continued. "Do you not recall that we fight God's battle for justice? We do not attack. We defend. Is that not true?"

"And if we have nothing to defend ourselves with?" Dumont asked.

"But we have guns, Gabriel, from the stores at Duck Lake and from the Mounted Police themselves."

"A small number, yes, but not enough. Half of our men have only old muskets, and some have nothing more than bows. Do you think we can defend our homes with these? Crozier is wise in the way battles are fought here on the prairies. A delay gives him plenty of time to plan."

"It is my belief," Riel said, "that there will be no need to fight at all. They must be willing to heed our complaints now that we have shown our will."

Dumont struggled to keep calm. "Louis, I know nothing of politics, but I have observed how much is accomplished with petitions. If we stop the Mounted Police's march now, we can take Prince Albert ourselves. When that happens, Battleford will follow and we will be masters of our own land. Then we will be strong and can deal face-to-face with the government of Canada." He banged the table with his fist. "It is a good plan."

Riel sighed. "Gabriel, it may seem to you it is a good plan; but it is not God's plan."

"You are certain you know what God's plan is, Louis?" Edouard broke in.

"It is you who came to Montana for me, but even before that I heard God's call. I must do his bidding."

Dumont's shoulders slumped. "Red Eagle, put away my horse. I find I do not need him."

Riel left and, as the door closed behind him, Edouard turned to his brother. "Do you believe him, Gabriel? Why would God choose such a one to lead us on the right path and not Father André or Father Vegreville?"

"It is what I ask every day," Tante Madeleine said. "Why do you believe in him?"

It was late afternoon, and in the slowly dimming light Ben thought the Métis general suddenly looked very old. "I must believe," he almost whispered, "or all has been for nothing."

Tante Madeleine looked at her husband with unseeing eyes and clutched her shawl around her shoulders tightly. "Louis Riel may be a prophet, but one need not be a prophet to know trouble approaches with long footsteps."

THIRTEEN

As spring unfolded, Ben often awakened to the crackle of river ice breaking up in huge chunks to move sluggishly downriver. He would lie awake then as a succession of worries chased through his head.

From a distance Métis scouts had watched the evacuation of Fort Carlton and later, even while some of the buildings had burned, the scouts had managed to retrieve most of the blankets and food the troops had been unable to carry. It was first thought that the Mounted Police commissioner had ordered the fire, but Riel's spies reported it had been started accidentally by a careless Hudson's Bay clerk. They also reported that Clarke had demanded all the company's stock be transported and guarded by the police, but he had been ignored.

In the April days that followed, Dumont's wound healed quickly, and Ben saw his eyes regain their twinkle as he teased his wife. The first two weeks of the month were spent readying the farm for planting. Red Eagle and Ben cleaned the barn and sheds while Dumont sharpened the plough and axes. At the end of the day, after the evening meal, they walked down to the little store beside the ferry and played billiards, sometimes with neighbours who dropped in to repeat the latest rumour from Prince Albert, Battleford, or Winnipeg. Dumont never commented and hardly seemed to listen. Nor did he go to church in Batoche with Tante Madeleine. When she bitterly told him that Riel had openly proclaimed himself the chosen delegate of the Holy Spirit and that Rome had been deposed, Dumont merely shrugged. He no longer seemed interested in the affairs of his people.

Almost half of April had passed when, during the noon meal, two men burst into the cabin to cry out that Indians had killed the agent and the priests at Frog Lake and made prisoners of the rest of the people there. After they left, Tante Madeleine turned to her husband. "This is Riel's work?"

Dumont reached for her hand. "No, I am sure it is not. As you know, he is against attacking forts and wishes the fight only to be in defence of Batoche."

"What happens now?" Ben asked.

Dumont struggled into his coat and reached for his rifle. "I will go myself to Batoche. It may be late when I return." When Ben and Red Eagle rose, he shook his head. "Stay here and take care of our place. If I do not return by tomorrow night, come to Batoche."

The following night Dumont returned in time for the evening meal. His face was grave. "There was more from the telegraph. Fort Pitt has been burned."

"By the same men?" Red Eagle asked. "From what reserve?"

"The same," Dumont said. "Do not fear. None were Poundmaker's people. They were warriors from the Big Bear Reserve far to the west."

"What about the women and children in the fort?" Tante

Madeleine asked. "The chief factor there has nine children."

"They may be safe. The Mounted Police were few, and the fort was not made for defending. The factor asked the police to leave so there would not be a fight and the people could go under Big Bear's protection. Big Bear is still chief, and it is believed the men who did this may have killed against his wishes."

"Did the Mounted Police get away all right?" Ben asked.

"During the night, they slipped away on an old barge."

Ben shivered. Two weeks ago the river still had plenty of ice.

"What will happen now?" Charity asked, her voice quavering.

Tante Madeleine's arm encircled the girl's waist, and her tone was cheerful as she said, "Perhaps nothing, *chérie*. Perhaps something good. The Canadians may at last give us attention. Do not worry. We have had our share of trouble before and survived very well."

Ben saw the pride in Dumont's eyes as he smiled at his wife. His face was no longer grave as he outlined his plans. "We have twenty head of cattle in the east pasture. We will bring them down tomorrow and slaughter two so our ladies may dry the meat. The rest we will drive to the Beardy Reserve. We will leave two there for the people to eat." He looked at Red Eagle and added, "In return I hope they will allow two or three of their men to help you drive the rest to a reserve just north of Waterhen Lake. I have cousins there who will keep them for me."

"What about me?" Ben asked. "I can help drive the cattle."

"No, my son. You will come back here with me when we get them to the Beardy Reserve. After what has taken place at Frog Lake, there may be other young warriors who wish to see the blood of white men."

Ben returned from the Indian camp feeling depressed and uneasy. When Charity asked how long Red Eagle would be away, he snapped, "How should I know? With all this craziness going on he might never get back." Charity's head jerked back as though Ben had struck her, making him even unhappier. "I'm sorry, Charity. It's just that I'm worried about him and everything else, and I guess I wanted you to feel as bad as I do."

She reached out until she felt his arm, then spoke with surprising firmness. "Ben, you know this is going to be over one way or another very soon. Tante Madeleine said so. After it's over, we'll go back to making the best we can out of our lives. The important thing is, we'll all do it together."

"I guess you're right like you almost always are. And to get back to what you asked, Red Eagle promised he'd be here as soon as he could, but he's got more'n fifty miles to cover. Even at a fast clip it'll take him three or four days to get to Waterhen Lake. Without the cattle on the way back, he'll be able to travel faster, but even so it might take three days. That's a whole week, Charity."

Eight days passed before Red Eagle returned. He found Ben piling brush in front of the rifle pits near the ferry at Batoche. "Ben, I have heard there has been a battle and a great victory for us. Tell me about it."

Ben dropped a pile of branches he had cut from newly leafed willow bushes and wiped his face with his shirttail. "It was some fight, all right. I tagged along before Gabriel had a chance to tell me not to. In some ways we won. It's hard to tell about a battle right off—everything happens so fast. First thing after we left you at the Beardy Reserve, we came back and loaded a wagon with all the stuff we could—food, clothes, books—and put it in the barn in case we had to leave fast. And we left a lot sooner than we thought we would. Two days later word came that a whole army was on its way. Not Mounted Police—a regular army with a general to give orders and a Gatling gun. That's a gun that fires so fast you think it's a hailstorm—maybe a hundred rounds a minute!" Then we brought all our stuff here. Gabriel wanted to attack the army before it got a chance to set up, but—"

"You do not need to tell me." Red Eagle grimaced. "Riel got divine word we must make our stand here at Batoche."

"That's right. Gabriel told him the men are getting plenty mad waiting while this General Middleton and his army strut across land they've been hunting on all their lives, so finally Riel said they could have a little skirmish. But nothing serious. That's when Gabriel picked Tourand's Coulee for an ambush."

"Tourand's Coulee?"

"A deep ravine near Fish Lake that runs from Tourand's farm to the river."

"How did Gabriel know the army would be there?"

"Henry, the freighter, got word to us. He drives a wagon for the army now and spies for Gabriel." Ben felt his heart pump faster as the scene flashed in his mind. "Edouard and thirty men stayed here to guard Batoche, and Gabriel took the rest with him. It was a sight to see—Gabriel riding at the head of the men, and the Cree and Sioux and the Salteaux all on the same side for a change and singing their war songs.

"Riel rode right up front with Gabriel, so it slowed things down some because he had to keep stopping to say the rosary. Finally we got to the Goulet farm and camped. About midnight some farmer rode by and said the Mounted Police were coming by the Qu'Appelle road to attack Batoche. Gabriel didn't believe it, but even so Riel took about fifty of the men and came back here.

"Around daybreak a scout reported the army was coming—about eight hundred men. So Gabriel split up our fighters—half on each side of Fish Creek. We hid the horses and waited while Gabriel took twenty men ahead to have a look. One of the army lookouts got too close to them and was shot, and that started everything. Gabriel told me he had one good shot at the general, but missed him and killed his hat instead. He barely made it back to where we were hiding. A story went around that Gabriel had been killed, so a whole lot of our men just left. We ended up with about sixty on our side of the creek against four hundred riflemen."

"Were you afraid?" Red Eagle asked.

Ben considered the question for a moment, then said, "I guess there wasn't time to be afraid. First thing I knew it was near sundown and we were running out of loads for the rifles. Gabriel set fire to the grass to make smoke, figuring he could sneak through it and get some guns off the bodies of the soldiers. He found three rifles and some ammunition, but while he was gone the Sioux left. Guess they figured Gabriel ran away. I tell you, Red Eagle, I thought it was the end. We were that short of men. Gabriel told me to get back to Batoche, but I just couldn't leave him there. Turns out Edouard heard the gunfire clear back here in Batoche and told Riel to sit down somewhere while he and the rest of our men came charging back on their horses. They tore right up the coulee and pushed the army back."

"How many did we lose?"

"All told four men, but we got thirty-two good army carbines and some other equipment the army left behind."

"And where is this army now?"

"Henry sent word that Middleton's waiting for reinforcements and supplies to come downriver on a steamer—the *Northcote*."

"And then they will come to Batoche. Where is Gabriel?"

"Up at headquarters. His wound got infected some, but Tante Madeleine's there to look after it. Charity, too."

Together they trotted up the slope to Letendre's house and found Dumont seated at the long table with Riel, Edouard, and a man Ben didn't recognize. Dumont rose to greet Red Eagle with a welcoming smile. "You are just in time. This man has news of Poundmaker."

The man was small and skinny, and his dark eyes darted from Ben to Red Eagle and back to Dumont before he said, "Yes, well, as I said, I am a trader and my cabin is at Breslayor. When I found out that Big Bear's warriors made trouble at Frog Lake, and later two Assiniboines killed a farmer, I thought it would be wise for me to camp for a time with my wife's people on Poundmaker's reserve. But they weren't there. Poundmaker had taken his people to see the Indian agent. I found them just before they reached Battleford."

When the man paused, Dumont said, "Poundmaker thought he should make the agent see for himself how his people suffer."

"That was not all," the man continued. "Poundmaker wanted to explain that not only his people, but all the Cree would be quiet again if they received better food and medicine and maybe some blankets. But only the blacksmith remained in Battleford. The whites were afraid when they learned so many Indians were coming, so they went to the fort for protection. The Indian agent sent a message for Poundmaker to come there to talk. He wanted to go, but his people were afraid he would be captured, so he waited outside the fort. But still the agent would not come out. A few Stoneys had joined Poundmaker on the journey and were hungry, so they broke into the empty stores. Soon after, many Cree did the same. Poundmaker tried to stop them, but they have been hungry and cold too long. I sat with him all night, and in the morning he scolded them and said they had to return to Cut Knife to wait for punishment."

"He should not return to Cut Knife!" Riel cried out. "He should bring his people here to aid our cause."

Dumont shook his head. "Poundmaker has listened to his friend Crowfoot, who has said he will not send the Blackfoot into battle again. The white men are well armed and there are too many to fight. He told Poundmaker, 'Even though our people may win one battle or many battles, they will suffer in the end as the Sioux have since Crazy Horse and Sitting Bull defeated Custer at Little Big Horn.' Perhaps he is right."

"I think Poundmaker does not have a choice," the little man retorted. "When I learned that Colonel Otter was marching to Cut Knife Hill with his army, I rode to meet him to explain that Poundmaker did not mean to make trouble. But the colonel would not listen. He intends to destroy Poundmaker once and for all."

Red Eagle turned abruptly and vanished through the open

doorway. Ben followed his friend as soon as he could excuse himself. He knew where to find Red Eagle, and walked uphill to the stable behind the house, pausing briefly at the foot of the rough ladder that led to the loft. When he climbed the ladder, he discovered Red Eagle stretched out on a bed of hay. "You asleep?" he asked.

Red Eagle grunted and sat up. "Not now."

Ben sat opposite the Cree. "Poundmaker will be all right. One of the reasons he's so respected by everybody is because he thinks everything through before he acts. He knows what he's doing."

"In the autumn when Poundmaker came to talk with Gabriel, I asked the chief when I should return to Cut Knife. I did not want to leave here, but I knew I should be with him, for he is truly my father. Poundmaker has looked into the future and sees that the numbers of our people grow less. He sees the white man learn more and more, and to survive we must do the same. Ben, he is happy we are friends and has asked one thing of me. No matter what happens to our band or to him, I am to stay by your side and learn as you do so that someday I may help our people." Red Eagle's voice dropped almost to a whisper. "I promised him I would do this."

Ben's chest tightened, and he had to clear his throat before he could reply. "That's what Charity and me want, too, Red Eagle. The three of us together. Here's my hand on it."

As they clasped hands, Red Eagle asked, "Does Gabriel believe we can fight an army so large?"

"He doesn't say, but I know this much. If he'd been allowed to go after that army the way he wanted, they'd still be running east." Red Eagle stared out the triangle of window, and Ben leaned forward to touch his shoulder. "Poundmaker knows what he's doing. He'll be just fine."

As if from far away, Red Eagle said, "I do not fear only for Poundmaker and the Cree, but for all of us."

FOURTEEN

In the days that followed, Dumont grew increasingly restless and irritable, and his arguments with Riel were almost a daily occurrence. When he learned that Middleton waited for reinforcements to arrive on the *Northcote* from Qu'Appelle, he became enraged. "Now, Louis," he demanded, "you see? We sit and do nothing instead of blowing up bridges and train tracks. We have men who hunger to tease these soldiers by bursts of gunfire at night so they cannot sleep. Had we shown our resolve, a thousand would have joined us. Right now we have only those from St. Laurent and the few who came from Fort à la Corne with Edouard. The others do not come forward because we cower here like sheep."

Riel shook his head and smiled at Dumont as a fond father does at an impetuous child. "Gabriel, how can you question the will of the Lord? He does not wish us to fight as Indians once did. Also, my general, has it occurred to you that some of the soldiers may be French Canadian?"

Dumont spat on the ground. "That is supposed to mean something to me when they come to take our land and destroy our lives?" When Riel didn't reply, Dumont said bitterly, "Perhaps under a flag of truce we could send word for those who are French Canadians to paint a fleur-de-lis on their face and we will blow kisses at them as they try to shoot us." He turned on his heel and strode off.

Ben and Red Eagle followed, and Dumont nodded at them, his anger already gone. "It is true if we wait much longer even the small number of Sioux and Stoneys will lose patience and leave us, and some of our people may return to their farms." His brow furrowed for a moment, then he said, "Perhaps our Henry who drives a wagon for this army has difficulty finding a way to get word to me, for I have heard nothing for three days. The enemy might be camped at Fish Creek still, but I would like to be certain. Tell Tante Madeleine to give you enough food for three days. I want you to return to our cabin and keep watch so that I will know when Middleton advances."

Ben's heart leaped. At last something to do besides dig pits and wait.

"Take care," Dumont warned, "for the enemy will have scouts, as well."

When they arrived at the cabin, it was cold and bare of all that had made it home. Although it was early afternoon, Ben and Red Eagle unrolled their blankets and stretched out to sleep, preferring to wait until dusk before they moved closer to the field force. Dumont had ordered them not to ride more than three miles from the cabin, halfway to where Fish Creek met the river. Closer would almost certainly risk capture by a patrol.

For two nights Ben and Red Eagle followed Dumont's

orders scrupulously and encountered nothing more than a coyote and the nervous rabbits it hunted. Emboldened, on the third night they left their horses hidden in a thicket and crept through the trees. They travelled above the river little more than a mile when they were startled to see smoke from campfires drift upward in the moonlight. When they heard the murmur of voices, they dropped to their bellies. Ben waited until his heart stopped thudding before he nudged Red Eagle and got to his feet. As he turned, he noticed the outline of a rifle barrel protruding from the shadow of the trees.

"Not a sound," a voice whispered as the rifle was lowered. "There's a sentry posted not fifty feet away. Come." When they hesitated, the voice added, "It's Henry, the freighter."

With Red Eagle on his heels, Ben stumbled after the freighter. When they were a safe distance downriver, Henry turned to face them. "Good thing I pulled guard duty tonight. I been trying to slip away to get word to Dumont. He send you to find me?"

With the danger of capture gone, Ben felt a wave of embarrassment; they had been found so easily. "I guess we're pretty lucky it was you that saw us."

The freighter grinned, then became serious. "Middleton's been waiting for the *Northcote* and the reinforcements. Got that Gatling gun on it, too. Now that it's here, he figures to move on, but it could take a month of Sundays. He's that afraid of ambushes after what happened at Fish Creek. Seems, though, his officers convinced him there aren't too many places downriver for Dumont to try that again. To make sure, he's sending the *Northcote* ahead to meet him at Gabriel's Crossing, and after that, Batoche."

"We camped out at the Crossing to watch," Ben said. "Guess we can go back and report to Gabriel now."

Henry nodded. "Tell him Middleton's really worried about how many men we got at Batoche. He figures he's outnumbered."

"How many does he have?" Red Eagle asked.

"All told about eight hundred, with more to come."

"Whew!" Ben said. "Wish we could count on more to come."

Henry got to his feet. "Me, too. Maybe Poundmaker's warriors will get to Batoche in time. Middleton just got word they whipped the tail off Otter and his men at Cut Knife Hill."

Red Eagle grasped Henry's shoulder. "Was Poundmaker wounded?"

Henry shook his head. "The way I heard it few Cree were hit at all. They slipped around in the ravines and had Otter's men trapped in a crossfire. They could've wiped out his whole army if they'd followed when Otter ordered a retreat, but Poundmaker rode up and down at the bottom of Cut Knife Hill, telling his warriors to stop. His war chief was afraid Poundmaker would get hit, so he called for a cease-fire."

It was the first time Ben had been alone in the Dumonts' cabin, and it seemed alien now—silent and bare after Red Eagle left for Batoche to repeat Henry's words. With the first sight of the field force or the *Northcote*, Ben was supposed to follow. Although bone-tired from too little sleep for the past few days, he found himself jumping at the slightest scrape of a branch on the cabin roof or the squeak of one of the mice in residence now that Tante Madeleine had left her home.

Near dawn Ben fell asleep, but at mid-morning he awoke with a start when he heard the rasp of wood sliding off wood. Snatching up his rifle, he opened the door a crack and looked toward the river.

The *Northcote* had bumped the landing.

Blood pounding in his ears, Ben yanked on his boots and dashed into the kitchen. Cautiously he opened the creaking shutters on a narrow window and lowered his rifle to the ground. Then, squeezing through, he dropped hands first into a row of flowers, flattened himself against the cabin wall, slid sideways, and peered around the corner.

Ropes were stretched from the boat to the landing, and a gangplank had been lowered. Ben took a deep breath, bent almost double, and raced to the shelter of the barn. He considered his situation. If there were no horses onboard, even if they spotted him, he would have no problem escaping once he was mounted. There were trees close to the barn, and beyond them the open prairie was out of rifle range. But then he remembered the Gatling gun, and his jaw tightened.

Horse saddled, he unlatched the side door that opened into the small fenced pasture partially hidden by two giant cottonwoods. There was a gate, but it faced the river, as did the big doors of the barn, and would bring him closer to the enemy. Ben glanced down at the river as he slowly led the horse from the barn. Men were moving along the gangplank now and up to the ferry house. Taking a deep breath, he swung into the saddle and gave his mount a smart crack on the hindquarters with the ends of the reins. The horse galloped in a wide circle before Ben turned it to face the back fence. His heart hammered. As far as he knew, the young mare had never jumped a fence. He kicked her once in the ribs. As she leaped forward, he felt her rise beneath him. For a long moment they seemed suspended between earth and sky before the landing jarred his spine. Without pausing he urged the excited animal into the grove of mixed spruce and aspen above the pasture, then turned to see if they had been observed.

Trees blocked his view, but the absence of gunfire and shouts encouraged him to bring his horse to a halt inside the woods. He slid to the ground, fastened the reins to a stout sapling, and crept to the edge of the trees.

Scanning the riverbanks as far as he could, he observed no evidence of the advancing army. But soldiers were still pouring from the *Northcote* and up the bank to the cabin as well as to the ferry house. He heard laughter as four of them emerged with Dumont's beloved pool table. There was a crash followed by the screech of wood ripped from the walls, and soldiers plodded from the cabin with planks to the *Northcote* where waiting hands hammered them along the rail for barricades. Heartsick, Ben watched two men lift Tante Madeleine's washing machine and carry it to the boat. Her stove went, too, before they turned their attention to the partly built house on the hill. Its walls fell quickly and were transported to the boat.

Ben had seen enough. He moved back to his horse stealthily and mounted it. As he turned the animal's head to make his way through the woods, he looked back. Fire poured from both the ferry house and the cabin.

When Ben returned to Batoche, he found Dumont in the church outside the village. The Métis commander had won at least one argument with Riel. The line of defence wouldn't be in Batoche itself. A chain of rifle pits had been dug south of the church and also between it and Mission Ridge on the river. Tante Madeleine seemed untroubled as Ben described the scene at Gabriel's Crossing. When he finished, she turned to her husband. "All we hold dear is here. The rest we will replace later."

Dumont nodded. "True, *chérie*, but I would still like to find a way to wreak vengeance on the *Northcote*."

As Ben listened to Dumont, he had a sudden inspiration. There might indeed be a way to put an end to the threat from the men on the *Northcote* and the gun it carried. "Gabriel, I've got an idea. The *Northcote*'s coming downriver ahead of the field force. Batoche's ferry cable is up high now so big boats can pass under. But what if we lower it a bit?"

Dumont's face lit up as he grabbed Ben's arm. "Do so. Red Eagle, cross the river on your horse, but take care. The water runs swiftly. Some of our men are in rifle pits over there, and they will help you lower the cable. We will do the same here." Giving Red Eagle a gentle push, he added, "Return quickly."

When the *Northcote* rounded the bend, the men onboard seemed oblivious to the rifle fire along both sides of the bank as the boat rapidly bore down on the landing. The helmsman saw the drooping cable and tried to turn, but it was too late. The cable tightened and slipped up and over the boat's bow to flatten the helm and tear off the smokestack. As the *Northcote* listed drunkenly, fire broke out and it disappeared downstream.

The cheer that rose from the men in the rifle pits was cut short when a scout on horseback thundered past. "They are here!" he called. "The army is here!"

Without permission from Dumont, Red Eagle and Ben raced to Mission Ridge, a plateau between the church and the river. They crouched in one of a line of pits, each connected to the other, and thrust the barrels of their rifles through the mounds of brush used as camouflage. "Do not waste your shots," Dumont called to his men from a nearby pit. "Aim with care. We must save our ammunition."

Hidden in the trees behind the church were more Métis, as well as Sioux and Cree, whose own rivalries were forgotten as they waited for their common enemy. Ben tried to swallow, but his mouth was too dry. A solid wall of soldiers appeared on top of the hill. When a bugle sounded, they halted. Then a large man in a fancy uniform moved forward on a white horse and trained a spyglass on the river.

"He looks for the *Northcote*," Red Eagle said. "The brave general wanted the boat to attack first."

There was no time to reply. The bugle sounded again, and men—some on horses, some on foot—swarmed down the hill, firing as they came. "They are many," Red Eagle said into Ben's ear when he stopped firing to reload.

Busy reloading his own rifle, Ben didn't reply. But he knew they were hopelessly outnumbered. Horses screamed and men sprawled in the dirt, but still they came. The spearhead of the attack had almost reached the church when he heard the war cries of the Sioux and the Cree and saw them sweep around it, firing guns and arrows from the backs of their horses. Caught in the crossfire between the Indians and the men in the pits, soldiers fell one after another. When the bugle sounded once more, they retreated up the hill. Métis leaped from rifle pits, cheering as they ran after the field force, sometimes dropping to one knee to fire and run again. Ben started to follow when he felt a hand grip his arm.

"No," one of the men said. "Gabriel calls us back. The Gatling gun speaks up there."

Even as the man said this, they heard the gun chatter. "I thought that weapon of the devil was lost with the *Northcote*," Red Eagle said.

Ben scowled. "They must have a pair of the blasted things. We better be certain Charity and Tante Madeleine are all right up there in the church."

When they reached the church, they found it crowded with women and frightened children huddled on benches and the floor. Father Fourmond, murmuring words of comfort, moved among them. His fringe of white hair, usually neatly combed, stuck out in all directions, and his eyes were rimmed with fatigue. He smiled faintly when Ben asked him where Charity and Tante Madeleine were. "They are in the rectory. Father Moulin has been wounded by a stray bullet."

With muttered thanks Ben and Red Eagle backed out of the church and raced next door. Three men lay on blankets close together in the small entryway, two with bandages on their heads and the other with a sling on his arm. They were given directions to a staircase and bounded up the steps two at a time. In a small room they found Tante Madeleine bent over a bed, tucking the covers around the white-bearded Father Moulin. The priest looked up as Ben approached, and his sad eyes brightened. Tante Madeleine turned and clasped both boys in her arms. "Tell me everything," she urged.

Ben's words rushed out as he assured her that Dumont was all right. In turn, he asked anxiously where Charity was. Tante Madeleine gestured to the doorway leading to the room that served as the priest's office. When Ben entered, he saw Charity sitting rigidly in a rocking chair, staring straight ahead. "Is that you, Ben?"

He grinned. "How'd you know?"

"We're twins, remember? Is Red Eagle here?"

The Cree moved quickly and knelt by her chair. "I am here"

Charity tried to smile. "Tell me what's happened. It's so hard to sit here doing nothing while you're outside maybe getting hurt."

From the other room Tante Madeleine said, "She was awake all night in the church helping to quiet the frightened children."

"They're on the run, Charity," Ben said. "If it weren't for that Gatling gun, we'd have them running all the way back to Winnipeg."

"But what about the cannon, Ben?" Tante Madeleine asked from the doorway. "We heard it far away and were concerned, but now we do not hear it."

Ben nodded. "I saw them haul one forward, but it must've misfired. We know they have two. They've been using them a lot to blow up all the houses they could along the river."

Tante Madeleine's lips tightened. "What kind of army makes war on houses?"

Ben had no answer. "Guess we better go. We'll tell Gabriel you're fine."

"Tell him I will have food ready for him down in the village. Riel's family is there, too."

Outside, sounds of sporadic firing drifted down the slope, even though the soldiers had retreated. A Métis hurried past, carrying a bucket. "They still fighting?" Ben asked.

The Métis paused and shook his head. "Enough only to create difficulties as they try to build their zareba."

"Zareba?"

The man waved a hand impatiently. "A barricade behind which to hide for the night. They use wagons, brush, and earth to protect the men and horses." He trotted off, but called over his shoulder, "I am looking for any ammunition the soldiers might have dropped. Even small rocks may be useful."

Ben was shocked. It didn't seem possible they could

be that short of ammunition. Suddenly he realized he had only two boxes of cartridges for his own rifle, and Red Eagle probably wasn't any better off. Together they followed the man.

Their search yielded little, for the older children of the village had scavenged the short grass as far up the hill as they dared. Ben and Red Eagle would have gone farther, but a Métis sentry barred their way. When it was too dark to see, they returned to the rectory. There was always tomorrow.

All night the men took turns, a few at a time, firing into the zareba to harass the enemy soldiers and keep them awake. The Indians in particular were eager for their turn. Their war cries from trees near the walls of the barricade echoed down the hill while they shot fire-tipped arrows inside to stampede the horses. Rolled in a blanket in a rifle pit, Ben wished grumpily they would stop long enough for him to get some sleep.

The sun rose, casting harsh, bright light. As the air warmed, the wind began to blow. Encouraged by their initial success, Dumont moved his men up to the rifle pits above Mission Ridge. This time Ben and Red Eagle were ordered to stay back. From the shelter of their own pit near the church, they saw the army attempt to move down the slope and heard Dumont's shouts to his men as he leaped from pit to pit. Each time the army surged forward, they were driven back, retreating at night with no more success than the day before.

In the gathering dusk, Dumont took Red Eagle and Ben aside. "I go to the rectory to sleep for a few hours, but first I have orders for you for tomorrow." He put a hand on Red Eagle's shoulder. "Today it goes well with us, but without more men and more guns we cannot hold out against so many. I am told Poundmaker comes, but slowly. I do not believe he will arrive in time, yet I bear my old friend no ill will. Each man must act upon that which he believes." He looked from Red Eagle to Ben. "I rely on my two sons to see that Tante Madeleine and Charity are safe. Sleep tonight in Batoche and, in the morning, take our wagon from Letendre's barn and drive it on the trail until it crosses the path to St. Laurent. On the left there is a wagon track into the trees. Hide the wagon there. If it does not go well for us, take Tante Madeleine and Charity to the wagon and I will find you. If I do not come, go on to my father's farm, which is not far from St. Laurent. Tante Madeleine knows the way. I will come later." He clapped a hand on the shoulder of each boy, then ducked into the rectory.

In the village Red Eagle and Ben rose with the sun. Without stopping to find food, they hitched the horses to the wagon, tied their saddled mounts behind, and started up the rutted track to the Carlton Trail. As they left Batoche, they saw other wagons loaded by women and children leave the village. By midday they had Dumont's wagon hidden in the trees and the horses staked nearby.

Avoiding the open trail, they led their mounts through the trees as they made their way back to the church. Red Eagle stopped suddenly and pointed east. Across the St. Laurent Trail the sun glinted off something metal. Silently they crept to the edge of the trees and looked up at the high plateau known as Jolie Prairie. There the sunlight bounced back from rifles carried by marching soldiers.

Ben was stunned. The field force was going to surprise the Métis by an attack from behind the church and their fortifications. Yanking on their bridles, they urged their horses forward. Less than a hundred yards on, they heard a familiar voice call their names. Startled, they halted and searched the trees. "Here, over here, Red Eagle, Ben. It's me, Henry. I been hit."

Cautiously they tied their horses and followed the sound of the voice. In a circle of scrub brush they found the freighter tying a kerchief around the calf of his leg.

"What happened?" Ben asked as they pushed aside the bushes.

Henry waved the question away. "Never mind me. They

saw me ride away and figured I deserted, so I got shot. My horse ran off. I got something for you to tell Gabriel."

Ben opened his mouth to speak, but Henry shook his head. "No, hear me. Middleton's moved a bunch of his men over on Jolie Prairie, knowing right well Gabriel would see 'em and most likely pull his men away from the river and ride to meet him. It's a trick. You gotta tell Gabriel that it's a trick and to pay no mind."

"You go," Ben said to Red Eagle. "I'll help Henry get to Tante Madeleine."

FIFTEEN

After Ben found Henry's horse and got the wounded man to the rectory, he learned that Red Eagle had reached Dumont almost too late. The bulk of the Métis fighters had started toward Jolie Prairie, and Middleton's army was poised to ride down on the weakened defences near the church. Most of the little fighting force had whirled their horses and galloped back to their comrades just in time to beat off the advance of the soldiers. Once again the general gained no ground.

Long before dawn the wind rose again to buffet the tents behind the church and make it impossible to build fires for morning tea. The weary Métis rolled from their pallets grumbling until Tante Madeleine and two other women called out. They had been busy inside the rectory. When they appeared with pots of tea and platters heaped with *galettes*, or cakes, the mood of the men improved. Some of them even joked about the possibility that the field force had been blown from the hill by the wind.

"Impossible," one old fighter declared. "Middleton is much too fat."

Beside Red Eagle in the shelter of the church, Ben attempted to laugh with the other men, but the laughter stuck in his throat. He tried to blame his increasing dread on the inescapable, dreary wind. But it was more than that. It was seeing each man finish his tea and dip into the pails under the eaves of the church to fill his pockets with nails and small stones. Still, he tried to joke. "I don't expect they'll try to attack us today. With wind this strong the bullets might blow back in their faces."

Ben was wrong. The wind increased with the coming of daylight, but before the sun was high the lookout in the church tower shouted down a warning. "On Jolie Prairie!" he cried. "They are on Jolie Prairie!"

The cry was repeated from pit to pit until Dumont galloped up to the church. Before his horse slid to a halt he was out of the saddle and inside. Men on horseback rode from the trees, rifles in hand, and gathered beside the church. Ben tried to look east in the direction of Jolie Prairie, but the sunlight blinded him. His heart pounded as he waited.

"It is not a ruse," Dumont reported when he climbed down from the steeple. "Through the spyglass I can see many soldiers. Middleton may want us to believe he is feinting again. We must be prepared." He pointed to each of his captains in turn and gave orders. Half the men were to ride to the trees across the trail from the soldiers gathering on the plateau. Those in the rifle pits on Mission Ridge and around the churchyard were to spread out to make up for the men leaving for Jolie Prairie.

"We go with you?" Red Eagle asked Dumont.

The harried leader shook his head. "No. Now is the time for you to obey the orders I gave you. Go to the church and care for Tante Madeleine and Charity. The men of Batoche have made arrangements with their families, as well, so you must tell all the women and children in the church it is time to leave. If we are successful today, they will return to the church. If we are not, the men will find them just as I will find you."

"But—" Ben began.

Dumont waved him silent. "Do not delay, my son. I will know if my family is captured and will come for you. If you are careful, this will not happen."

Ben tried to rid himself of the painful lump in his throat as he watched Dumont wheel his horse, one hand clutching Le Petit, and lead a pitifully small number of badly armed men—Indian and Métis—around the church and into the trees.

"Many have left their rifles and have taken old muskets," Red Eagle said. "All they have to shoot are nails and stones."

"Your people, too, Red Eagle. It takes some nerve to fight against repeating rifles and nine-pounders with bows and arrows."

Red Eagle smiled, but his eyes were filled with pain. "They are men again and take orders from their chiefs instead of government men. And the chiefs are proud. For now."

With dread Ben followed Red Eagle into the church. This wouldn't be easy. He knew Tante Madeleine wouldn't want to leave the wounded. Added to that, he was afraid the women and children might panic when they were told they had to hide in the woods.

Frightened they might have been, but the mothers and grandmothers of the children calmly set about packing the few possessions they had brought with them when they had taken refuge in the church. Most were determined to walk back to their homes in Batoche to gather more belongings before they went to the woods behind the village to hide. Since there was no sound of gunfire yet, neither Ben nor Red Eagle argued with them. Tante Madeleine was another matter, however, and it took the combined efforts of Red Eagle, Ben, and Father Moulin to convince her the priests, with the help of a prisoner or two, could look after the wounded men for one day.

Once she agreed, Tante Madeleine gathered the clothing she had brought for her family and prepared a bag of food. "Not too much," Ben cautioned. "There's only two horses—one for you and one for Charity. The other pair are with the wagon."

Ben was aware Charity hadn't said a word yet and wondered if she was too scared to talk. He looked at her carefully when she emerged from the church and was relieved to see that Tante Madeleine had made her dress sensibly. He recognized a pair of his own outgrown britches under the heavy dark blue hooded cloak. When she laughed as Red Eagle led her to the horse and said she was a boy now, too, Ben relaxed. Charity would be just fine.

As Ben helped Tante Madeleine mount the other animal, one of the nine-pounders boomed in the distance. With his hand gripping the bridle, it took all his strength to keep the horse from bolting. Charity's mount was less nervous, but Red Eagle kept a firm grip on its bridle as he half walked, half ran behind Ben and Tante Madeleine. Facing the shrieking wind, they swung in a wide circle away from the church until they entered the dense mix of spruce, cottonwood, and fir and paused to take deep, gulping breaths.

In the protection of the trees the wind dropped, but their rest was short-lived, for not more than a hundred yards on their right Dumont's men responded to the guns from Jolie Prairie. Ben clutched the bridle again and started through the trees, his ears picking out the different sounds of gunfire. The rifles of the soldiers spat endlessly farther away, but there were few reports from rifles among the Métis. More often he heard the defiant challenge of the muskets throwing out their collection of stones and nails.

Ben could stand it no longer. "Wait here a minute," he said to Red Eagle. As his friend reached for the bridle of Tante Madeleine's mount, Ben dashed through the trees. Closer than he thought, he found one of the men from St. Laurent crouched behind a pile of downed timber. Responding to his frantic gestures, Ben dropped to his knees beside him.

"You have shells, no?" the Métis asked, eyes hopeful.

Ben pulled five from his jacket pocket. His last seven he kept for himself. He had Tante Madeleine and Charity to protect.

Clearly the Métis was disappointed, but he managed a faint grin and said, *"Merci."*

Over the pile of trees and the bushes beyond, directly opposite, Ben could see puffs of smoke as the soldiers fired across the St. Laurent Trail. He rubbed his eyes; the enemy seemed to be advancing slowly to the very edge of the plateau.

The Métis cursed under his breath. "I think they are trying to trick us again. I can hear plenty of gunfire back near the river."

Ben shaded his eyes and glanced in the direction of the zareba. It was hidden by trees and the hill itself, so he couldn't see it, but he was certain he could make out figures moving above the cemetery. Faintly he heard the cannon speak. Remembering his promise to Dumont, he backed away on his knees. "I'll return," he told the Métis, who aimed his rifle across the trail and nodded.

It took half the morning to work their way through the woods behind the church to reach the wide Carlton Trail. Because the forest on the other side hadn't been scavenged for fallen trees for the fires of Batoche, it was littered with aspen and fir, making it difficult to find the track where the wagon was hidden. The horses resented picking their way and hopping over logs, but it would be dangerous to expose themselves by following the open trail until it intersected with the one to St. Laurent. Impatiently Tante Madeleine swung off her horse. "I prefer to walk," she said, gathering her shawl closely about her shoulders as she pushed aside the bushes in front of her and led the way.

When they found the hidden wagon, Tante Madeleine immediately removed the family of mice nesting in the four blankets she had left behind. From the bag she had brought from the rectory she extracted *galettes* and meat. Red Eagle took a jug from the wagon and reappeared a few minutes later with water. Ben chewed the meat with enthusiasm and wished he wasn't always so hungry. It didn't seem decent somehow to eat when Dumont and the others were— Suddenly the food stuck in his throat. "I'll go back and see what's happened," he muttered. Then, without waiting for a response, he swung onto his horse.

Within minutes Ben reached the spot where the Métis had been firing from behind the logs, but it was empty. When he looked toward the plateau, he couldn't make out a single soldier, which filled him with desperate hope. Cautiously he guided his horse out onto the trail and turned its head into the wind. With a kick from his heels, Ben forced the animal to canter, then gallop. As he drew closer to the church, he swung his horse off the trail and followed a beaten path until he reached the rifle pits near the rectory. Looking around, he was overwhelmed with horror.

A horde of uniformed men lined the top of the hill, more joining as he watched. Below, the few men left to defend the southern flank were spread out thinly in the pits. There was no sign of panic as they waited in the eerie silence, broken only by the wail of the wind funnelling through the church tower.

Ben leaped from the saddle and cursed as he realized he had left his own gun behind. He ducked low as he scurried from pit to pit until he found a rifle beside a man who would never use one again. But it was empty. With shaking hands he fumbled in his coat pocket for the few cartridges he had left, then shook his head in disgust. They wouldn't fit the rifle he held. Beside him, a man he didn't know said, "If you don't need those shells, give them to me."

Wordlessly Ben handed them over, then ducked low again and returned to the pits closest to the rectory. When a hand struck his shoulder, he turned to see Dumont glaring at him. "You have disobeyed me. Where are Madeleine and Charity?"

"They're safe, Gabriel," Ben said. "I had to come back and see what happened to you."

Dumont's expression didn't soften. "You did wrong, Ben. Your duty is to look after our family." He smiled grimly. "However, I do have a use for you, but you must promise that when you are done you will not return to me but will go back to the woods."

Ben nodded, and Dumont continued. "Ride to Batoche. If there are women or children there, tell them to get out. After the next attack, we must fall back to the village and defend it as long as we can."

Darting from the pit, Ben raced behind the rectory. There, nervously cropping the daffodils Father Moulin had planted, was his untied horse. He leaped onto its back and, heedless of the enemy, galloped into the shelter of the trees. Without slackening speed, horse and rider crashed through the brush on a direct course to the tiny village.

The hoofs of his horse thundered up and down the quiet street as Ben shouted his warning. But there was no one to answer his cries. Satisfied the houses were empty, he turned the head of his mount away from the trail to the open fields and beyond them to the woods. On the edge of the forest he reined in his horse as the sound of a bugle floated above the wind. It was followed by spattering gunfire and the muted roar of voices.

Even though despair blurred his vision, Ben could see the North-West Field Force sweeping down the hill toward the waiting Métis.

SIXTEEN

It was late when a weary Ben returned to Charity and the others. In spite of his urging, Tante Madeleine was inflexible. "We must wait for Gabriel," she said firmly. "If it should take a week, we will wait for him. He will come."

Hesitantly Ben reminded her that Dumont himself had ordered them to go to his father's home if he didn't return by nightfall, and it was now near midnight. "I'd rather wait, too," he admitted. "But he expects us to do what he tells us."

"No," Tante Madeleine said. She managed a smile, but in the lantern light her eyes were circles of sorrow. "Gabriel knows I would not leave without being certain he is safe."

Charity touched his arm. "Don't plague Tante Madeleine, Ben," she whispered. "Likely we're safer hidden in the woods than we'd be on the road, and we have to find out what's happened to Gabriel."

Ben gave up and decided to take a walk to keep warm. Nearly a dozen others from the village had found their way into the woods around them, and Tante Madeleine had given their blankets to the children, keeping only one for Charity. He rose from his seat on the frigid ground and swung his arms back and forth. His whole body stiffened when a hand seized his arm from behind and whirled him around. Dumont!

Tante Madeleine rushed forward and was swept up in a bone-crushing embrace. They all whispered at once, but Dumont silenced them and drew his wife down to sit beside him on a log. "I will not deceive you. It goes badly for us. Even now the soldiers search for those who escaped before they captured Batoche."

"Did many get away?" Ben asked.

Dumont nodded. "On the high ground, with only six of our brave fighters, we held off that well-fed general for an hour. Time enough for the rest to get away. Riel wanted all of us to surrender, but I said no. We must live to fight another day. I will talk with him tomorrow."

"No," Tante Madeleine said fiercely. "You will leave here now and I will follow."

Dumont stroked her head with a big hand. "Not yet, *chérie*. I must try to persuade Riel to come with me." His eyes searched the wagon. "It is cold. Where are your blankets?"

"There are children in these woods without blankets, Gabriel," Tante Madeleine said.

Dumont rose and picked up Le Petit. "Come with me," he ordered Ben.

The big man moved silently through the trees so rapidly that Ben could scarcely keep the outline of his bulky figure in front of him without making noise himself. His legs were beyond tired, and when Dumont halted abruptly Ben's knees buckled and he sank to the ground.

"Rest," Dumont whispered. "I must go on alone."

In less than ten minutes he returned to whisper, "Two soldiers guard one big tent. It holds what they took from us, so it follows we should take it back."

Numbly Ben got to his feet and followed to the edge of the trees. The moonlight illuminated the big tent half hidden behind the church. It was guarded by two soldiers—one in front and one in back. "We wait," Dumont breathed in Ben's ear, pointing upward. The wind had diminished to a breeze near the ground, but high above, the clouds scudded swiftly across the sky. A long bank of fleecy white approached the face of the moon, and when it cut off the light and plunged the ground into darkness, Dumont said, "Wait here."

Ben was alone.

The clouds still hid the moon when Dumont returned minutes later, leading two horses. As he tied them to a tree, he said over his shoulder, "Come."

In a half crouch they darted from the trees to the tent where Ben almost fell over the body of a soldier. There was no time to think about him, for Dumont pulled Ben inside and loaded his arms with blankets.

The sun was high when Ben woke the next day. He had been warm all night, wrapped in the thick Hudson's Bay blanket atop a mound of pine boughs. Beside him, Red Eagle sat up and stretched mightily. Dumont was perched on a fallen spruce, cleaning his rifle, but Tante Madeleine and Charity were nowhere in sight.

"Bon jour!" Dumont called softly. "Our ladies have found a stream to wash their pretty faces in." He slipped from the log and moved closer to Ben and Red Eagle. "I must leave to find Riel, for we have much to say to each other."

"Will you be back?" Ben asked.

"*Oui*, but not here. I spoke of this with Tante Madeleine and she agrees we should meet at my father's house. There we will make plans."

"What about the soldiers looking for us?" Ben asked.

"It is best for you to speak the truth as much as possible. If you go up the trail boldly as though you have nothing to hide, they may not stop you. You are young and not Métis. Red Eagle is your friend. Still, it might be wise also to inform them your uncle is chief factor for the company and justice of the peace."

"What about Tante Madeleine?" Red Eagle asked.

"Tante Madeleine is not concerned. Now," Dumont said, gesturing behind him, "my horse is there and I must go." He waved Le Petit in salute.

Tante Madeleine drove the wagon, with Charity beside her, while Ben and Red Eagle rode behind. A string of a half-dozen wagons followed, crowded with sad-eyed women and silent children. One by one the other wagons turned into clearings to be welcomed on farms owned by relatives or friends. By late afternoon Tante Madeleine's was the only wagon left.

When they turned from the St. Laurent Trail onto the double track that led through the trees to Isidore Dumont's farm, Ben relaxed, believing they hadn't been discovered by soldiers or police. Less than a mile into the woods, however, they came face-to-face with Superintendent Crozier and a dozen of his men.

"Bonsoir, madame," the policeman said, nodding at Tante Madeleine. Then, turning to Charity, he said, "And good evening to you, too, Miss Charity." When he looked at Red Eagle and Ben, he regarded them with hard blue eyes.

Ben knew it was useless to fabricate a story for this man's benefit, and before he could be asked, he blurted, "The soldiers burned Tante Madeleine's house, so we're taking her to Isidore Dumont's place."

"My men and I have just come from there," Crozier said, looking away for a long moment. When he gazed at Tante Madeleine again, his face had softened. "For the burning of your house I'm truly sorry, madame. If General Middleton had listened to the Mounted Police, we might have avoided this sad ending."

Tante Madeleine studied the trees as though she hadn't heard.

"Madame," the superintendent continued politely but firmly, "as you may know, we're looking for Gabriel Dumont and Louis Riel. It'll go better for them if you can persuade them to surrender to us before they're found by the army."

Slowly Tante Madeleine turned her head. A moment later she smiled. "Superintendent Crozier, if you and the government of Canada and the big army cannot make Gabriel Dumont do what he does not wish, how do you expect me, a mere woman, to achieve this?"

Without replying Crozier turned from her to the two boys. Ben waited, wondering what would come next. Crozier might be a bit sympathetic, but if the man knew he had been responsible for spiking his cannon at Duck Lake, no amount of sympathy would help. Possibly the superintendent didn't know, for his expression wasn't stern when he motioned Ben to follow him out of earshot of the others.

Crozier reached inside his tunic and brought out a sealed packet. "Your uncle is ill and took his family south. He asked me to give you this. I believe there's a letter inside."

Uncle Lawrence! Ben had almost forgotten about him. "Thanks. I'll read it later.

Crozier cleared his throat. "This has been a sorry business, and Lawrence Clarke had a part in it, but I believe him to be a man of principle. He seemed certain his efforts would protect both the company he served and the people here—Indians and Métis alike."

"I expect you're right," Ben said after a moment's pause.

Crozier reached over awkwardly and touched Ben on the shoulder. "It doesn't matter if others might disagree with me, but each man must do what he believes to be right. I suspect you learned that for yourself, Ben"

As the superintendent studied him, Ben felt his ears redden. Did that remark carry a double meaning? Abruptly the policeman added, "I suppose even if you knew, you wouldn't reveal the whereabouts of Dumont or the others?" When Ben didn't reply, Crozier turned his horse "Then there's nothing more to be said."

Ben took a deep breath and blew it out as Crozier nodded to Tante Madeleine and Charity, then signalled his men to follow him up the track.

When they arrived at Isidore's small cabin, they found two rooms packed with furniture and tools. Both the very old man and his much younger wife welcomed them warmly, but Ben sensed Tante Madeleine was ill at ease.

"It's very hard for her to be comfortable in the home of another woman," Charity explained as she and Ben washed their hands and faces in the basin on a bench outside. "Ben, promise we won't leave until Gabriel comes? I'd feel ever so much better if I were sure she wouldn't have to stay here for a long while. When Ben didn't answer, Charity felt for his arm. "Ben?"

A thought had occurred to him, and with her touch a grin broke over his face. "Charity, I just got the best idea. Wait here until I get Red Eagle. We got something important to talk over."

The woods around the cabin had grown dark, and there were only traces of gold on the horizon when Dumont returned two nights later. Red Eagle and Ben sat on the ground under an ancient spruce tree, making plans for their journey to the farm on the Red River. Red Eagle stopped Ben's words with a hand on his arm. "Listen. He is here."

The high, sweet trill of a red-winged blackbird floated from the trees. Ben stared at his friend. "All I hear is a bird."

The Cree scrambled to his feet. "A bird that has not yet arrived for the summer."

Inside the forest two big hands reached out to them. "It is safe?" Dumont asked. They nodded and he grinned.

As soon as they entered the cabin, Red Eagle and Ben kept

watch through windows on each side, while Dumont sat at the long table and wolfed down deer steak and potatoes. After assuring his father that his brother, Edouard, was safe, Dumont said, "I found Riel in the woods, but I cannot persuade him to go south with me. We lost a dozen good men and some are prisoners. It is his wish to be one or the other, and the same for me. He will surrender tomorrow."

Beside him, Tante Madeleine cried out. "Gabriel, you cannot surrender!"

Dumont squeezed her hand. "*Non, chérie*. If not for you, I would not care what happens to me now. As it is, I go to Montana where many of our people settled after they were cheated out of their land in Manitoba. Perhaps they will aid me in finding help for our people here. Later I will send for you."

The big man put down his wooden spoon and stared into the distance as he continued. "I go with a burden on my soul. My friends and brother Isidore died in this fight, and many Métis children are without homes." He took a deep breath. "I have much love for our people, but have done them great harm."

Over the chorus of denials Dumont's father shouted, "The blame is Louis Riel's! If you had led the men the way you wanted to, the army of that general would now be in small pieces."

Dumont shook his head. "Riel also cares much for our people. He was guided by visions, though I now think he did not understand what was meant by them. But it was Gabriel Dumont the men trusted to plan the battles well. For that I should have listened to myself. They should have been fought out on the prairie far from Batoche. I do not think we would have lost then, but if we had, perhaps our homes would not be destroyed."

Red Eagle turned away from the window. "Gabriel," he said haltingly, "what about Poundmaker and my people?"

A look of pain crossed the Métis leader's face. "I did not forget Poundmaker, Red Eagle. I was going to tell you later outside, but perhaps it is just as well now. Poundmaker sent two of his men to tell me that he will surrender to Middleton."

Red Eagle's fists were clenched by his sides as he cried out, "But he has done no wrong! My people were attacked and had to defend themselves."

"I know," Dumont said gently, "and for that he may be pardoned. Part of his message was to remind you of your promise not to return to Cut Knife."

His face an unreadable mask, Red Eagle turned back to the window.

Dumont mopped up the gravy on his plate with a bit of bread and swallowed it. *"Très bien,"* he said to his stepmother. Then he stood and reached for Le Petit. "It is time."

"We will walk with you a little way," his wife said.

Tante Madeleine ushered the young people outside so Dumont could bid goodbye to his father and stepmother alone. When he left the cabin, he reached for his wife's hand and started for the woods. Above the sheltering trees, the moon shot cold white shafts of light through the forest. Without them they wouldn't have seen the tall black horse pawing the ground impatiently. Dumont slid his rifle into the scabbard fastened to the saddle and turned to them.

Ben's mouth was almost too dry to speak, for it was possible Tante Madeleine would be angry with him. She had already made it clear that Dumont expected her to care for his ill father until he could send for her, and she would do nothing to disappoint her husband.

Swallowing hard, Ben said, "Gabriel, if you could wait a minute, we have something to ask." He cleared his throat. "Charity, Red Eagle, and me want to ask you if it's all right for Tante Madeleine to go south with us and wait for you on our farm on the Red River. We think she'd like that, but she won't even talk about it, because you want her to stay here with your father."

Before Dumont could reply, Ben hurried on. "I drew a map for you to find us. The farm's right on the Red River not far from where it joins the Assiniboine River. I expect the cabin's still standing. My pa took care building it. We have to buy supplies and stock, of course—"

"Please don't say no," Charity broke in. "I...we all need Tante Madeleine so much."

The moonlight sparkled on the tears that trickled from Tante Madeleine's eyes, but a smile lit up her face when Dumont put his arms around her and said, "I am an imbecile not to think of this myself." He released his wife and looked at her. "I ask but two days more so you may teach my father's wife how to care for him." He rummaged in his shirt pocket and took out a small packet. "It is fortunate Tante Madeleine removed our money from behind the chimney and brought it with her to Batoche."

"No, Gabriel," Ben protested. "We got more than we need. Uncle Lawrence left a letter with the papers showing we own the farm. He's sorry for a lot of things, and there was money in the letter, too, enough for us to get supplies for the trip and a bit of stock for the farm after we get there. I expect some of the money is what he got for our chickens and cows."

The big man reached out to hug Ben and Red Eagle, then turned to Charity and put a hand on each side of her face. "I will think of you all with my Madeleine as a family should be."

When the Métis leader swung into the saddle and turned his horse, Red Eagle moved closer and said softly so only Ben and Dumont could hear, "They say General Middleton has sworn he will find you."

Dumont grinned wickedly and patted his rifle. "*Bien.* I have sent this general a message. Le Petit has seven cartridges yet. Let him come find us."

As the first steps of the horse carried Dumont into the shadows, guilt overcame Ben. He couldn't stand it any longer. "Wait!" he called as loudly as he dared. The horse stopped, and with a glance at Red Eagle, Ben said, "Stay here. I'll be right back."

Dumont leaned from the saddle, listening to Ben's tumbling confession. When Ben fell silent, Dumont rubbed his bearded chin thoughtfully. "You agreed to tell Lawrence Clarke of events in Batoche so he would not order you and Charity back to the fort? And he would have you believe by doing that you helped the Métis?"

Miserably Ben nodded. "Even if nothing I told him made any difference, I did you a wrong. I should have told you about this a long time ago."

Dumont reached down, grasped Ben's shoulder, and shook it fondly. "That much is true. You should have told me. For out of nothing you have made a heavy burden. You must put it from your mind and think only of guiding our family safely to the Red River."

For a long time after the horse and rider melted into the blackness of the forest, the three young people waited while Tante Madeleine strained her eyes for a last glimpse of her departing husband. Finally Charity whispered, "Is it very far to Montana? He'll be all right, won't he, and after a while he can come back?"

"For sure, Charity," Ben said. "He knows every tree, stone, and river from here to Montana, and the army sure doesn't. You know Gabriel. He won't quit until he finds a way to help his friends here. He'll be back."

Heartened by his own words, Ben gently turned Tante Madeleine around, reached for Charity's hand, and said to Red Eagle, "Gabriel would be real upset if he thought we were standing around worrying about him when we should be making plans for that long ride to the Red River we got ahead of us."

As they moved toward the cabin, a thin shaft of moonlight lit the faces of Ben's companions and he was relieved to see there the same feelings of hope and anticipation that had arisen in his own heart. They were a family, he thought, and no matter what happened they always would be.